PULP Literature

PULP Literature

PULP LITERATURE PRESS

Issue No. 27, Summer 2020

Pulp Literature Press, Publisher; Jennifer Landels, Managing Editor; Mel Anastasiou, Senior Editor; Jessica Fabrizius, Editor; Genevieve Wynand, Acquisitions Editor; Daniel Cowper, Poetry Editor; Emily Osborne, Poetry Editor; Amanda Bidnall, Copy Editor and Graphic Designer; Mary Rykov, Proofreader; Samantha Olson, Assistant Editor; Veronica Kos, Assistant Editor; Carol McCauley, First Reader; Kate Landels, Cover Design. For advertising rates, direct inquiries to info@pulpliterature.com.

Cover painting, *Howe Sound Visitors* by Mel Anastasiou. Artwork for 'Linen, Leeks, and Blood' by Kris Sayer. All other illustrations by Mel Anastasiou.

Pulp Literature: ISSN 2292-2164 (Print), ISSN 2292-2172 (Digital), Issue No. 27, Summer 2020.

Published quarterly by Pulp Literature Press, 21955 16 Ave, Langley, BC, Canada V2Z 1K5, pulpliterature.com, at $15.00 per copy. Annual subscription $50.00 in Canada, $68.00 in continental USA, $86.00 elsewhere. Printed in Victoria, BC, Canada, by First Choice Books / Victoria Bindery. Copyright © 2020 Pulp Literature Press. All stories and works of art copyright © 2020 their authors as per bylines.

Pulp Literature Press gratefully acknowledges the support of the Canada Council for the Arts.

Pulp Literature is a proud member of the Magazine Association of BC and Magazines Canada.

TABLE OF CONTENTS

FROM THE PULP LIT PULPIT

A Time to Build Up

In magazine publishing, issues are planned months — even years — in advance. Peering deep into our editorial crystal ball, we look to the future, envisioning the final product that you will ultimately hold in your hands, the stories you will invite into your life, the fortunes you will want told.

Here at *Pulp Lit* we mark time by the steady tempo of the four seasons. An exercise in divination, we imagine the future while firmly planted in the present. And, as Ecclesiastes (and The Byrds) remind us, to everything there is a season and a time to every purpose.

As shufflers and gamblers of words, we selected these stories long before the portentous phrases — *quarantine, social distancing, self-isolation, shelter in place* — became our new deal with reality. We gazed into our crystal ball, cloudy and uncertain, and asked, *What will summer bring?*

In truth, not one of us ever really knows what the future holds. Publishing, like a crystal ball or shuffle of the deck, is all about taking a chance on the sweetness of life's persistent unfolding. But whatever the fates decide, be it sweet or sour, great stories allow us to conjure our own escape. And perhaps *that* is the most comforting fortune of all.

We hope these words find you safe and well, and reassured in knowing that as one season ends, a new one always begins.

~Genevieve Wynand

In THIS ISSUE

The intoxicating alchemy of *Howe Sound Visitors* by cover artist **Mel Anastasiou** blends the ephemeral and the enduring, a heady potion that infuses the stories within these pages.

Friends and lovers dance and slide through memory in 'Joran's Song' by **Dave Gregory** and 'The Lover Snake' by **Tomson Highway**.

Life finds a way in two very different post-apocalyptic worlds as **Jakob Drud** in 'Culinary Subjugation' and **Kim Harbridge** in 'Projections' take us under the dome.

Meanwhile, young and old experience the shapeshifting powers of perspective in 'Dead of Summer' by **R Daniel Lester** and 'Linen, Leeks, and Blood' by **Kris Sayer**.

And success comes down to the powers of persuasion in 'The Lion' by **Hannah van Didden** and 'Captain Hero was a Feminist' by **NRM Roshak**.

Emblematic of our genre-crossing ways, *Pulp* short-story alumni **Erin Kirsh** and **Peter Norman** return, this time with their words woven into poetry.

The hive is buzzing with anticipation for this year's Bumblebee Flash Fiction Contest stories! Winner **Kate Felix** claims the sweet top prize with 'Shayna's Eulogy'. And whoever said no to a second (or third!) scoop of honey? Runner-up **Kim Martins** with 'Let's Start with the Horse' and **Mitchell Toews** with 'Piece of My Heart' keep the delectable delights flowing.

The accolades continue as we bring you 'He Who Can Open All Doors' by **Crystal Bourque**, Honourable Mention for the 2019 Surrey International Writers' Conference Storyteller Award.

Perennial favourites Frankie Ray and Allaigna return in this issue. Frankie is poised for her big Hollywood chance in **Mel Anastasiou**'s 'Frankie Ray Stands Alone', and Allaigna's career takes a sudden leap after six years of military service in the new novella by **JM Landels**, *Allaigna's Song: Oburakor*.

Jes, Gen, Mel, Jen & Sam
Pulp Literature Press

Out of the fires of a Caribbean slave revolt, shipwrecked on the jungle coast of 16th-century Ecuador, an educated slave, a shaman, and a monk hunted by the Inquisition fight for freedom against the might of Imperial Spain.

Dive into an epic slipstream novel of intrigue and adventure from fantasy author Matthew Hughes, the writer George R.R. Martin calls 'criminally underrated,' and Robert J. Sawyer says is 'a towering talent.'

'A triumph!' - Cecelia Holland
'Sensational' - Candas Jane Dorsey

pulpliterature.com

Fantastic Fresh Fiction!

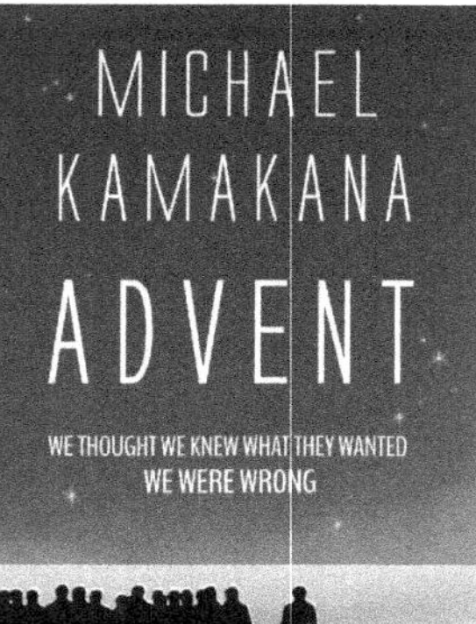

THE LOVER SNAKE

Tomson Highway

Tomson Highway is a Cree writer from northern Manitoba who also happens to be a classically trained pianist. As such, he writes music in addition to his plays and novels, music that comes out as songs which he performs in cabaret with singers and such, wherever and whenever he gets invited. What makes his writing unique in all these forms is that his mother tongue, Cree, figures largely; one almost always reads or hears it. 'The Lover Snake' was published in An Anthology of Canadian Native Literature in English (Oxford University Press), and predates most of his published work. You can find Tomson Highway's music on his website tomsonhighway.com.

$\mathcal{T}$HE LOVER SNAKE

The magazine photograph is of a Sikh. A male Sikh. Sikhs wear turbans. It's a tradition that goes back many, many generations, so it is said. You can always tell a Sikh when you see one by the turban he wears. Men, as I recall, also wear beards like this one in the photograph does. Fine beards. A fine-boned people. This particular Sikh, the man in the photograph, has, pictured with him, the uppermost portion of a large snake slithering down over the front and centre of the bright orange turban he wears, the reptile's diamond-shaped head, with its distended eyes, hovering just centimetres over the man's forehead, its flickering tongue slicing air between his eyes. This is the photograph in the magazine.

Dahljeet has always worn a turban, as I remember. In fact, he has an entire closet full of them at his home in Vancouver. Dahljeet is a Sikh.

Now Dahljeet and I have been friends for many years. An unusual alliance, people would observe from time to time. And between us, Dahljeet and me, we would agree that the friendship was an unusual friendship. I mean, there he was, very much an Indian and here I was, also very much an Indian. Only, we were such totally different kinds of Indian. Worlds apart. So different, it was laughable. And we'd laugh. North Cree hunter ambles down the slope of Robson Street beside north Indian maharajah. An odd pair. To be sure.

And yet, we became close, Dahljeet and I. More than friends, more than brothers, more than lovers, even. It was almost as if, in the midst of certain totally unexpected moments in time we spent together, there would arrive from somewhere a certain buzzing half-sound, a certain inner ringing as perfect in pitch and purity as the tone from a tuning fork. It was beautiful. We met when we were both just short of twenty years of age.

Dahljeet would talk of elephant parades at magnificent royal weddings in the heat and dust of not-so-long-ago north India and of dark women in rainbow-coloured saris, draped in silver and gold and diamonds at summer places in the mountains and at winter places away from mountains. He had stories, too, of cobras that I remember particularly well.

And me? Well, I would talk to him of pure white snow and of rivers that never run dry and of ice-cold lakes from which you could drink by simply dipping your hand through crystal surfaces and cupping and lifting water to your mouth. I talked—not to be outdone by his stories of elephant parades and gold-sprinkled saris—of vast herds of caribou in springtime, a sea of rolling, shifting, swaying antlers before my hunter father's keen, watchful eye. And of moccasins and belts covered with the most fanciful patterns and designs in glass beads. My sister, Marie-Adele, in particular, I'd confide to Dahljeet, is an artist at the art of applying beadwork to the smoked hide of young caribou. He owned twenty-seven turbans, my friend said in reply, and, later that afternoon, he showed me these twenty-seven turbans in his closet in his home in Vancouver: the colours were fantastic.

There are no snakes where I was born, so Weesageechak, that half-crazed little Cree Indian clown whom no one's ever seen, though he's lived ten thousand years and more among us, I told Dahljeet, this particular Weesageechak, well, he's never seen a snake or done anything with one or ridden one or cooked one and eaten one. He would have danced with one if he'd met one, I laughed. No. No snakes in far north Saskatchewan … which made his stories of maharajas and cobras, yes, cobras in particular, that much more fascinating. I was electrified!

They say, in north India, according to my friend, Dahljeet — he of the twenty-seven multi-coloured turbans and the fine, dark beard — that cobras mate at a certain time in their lives, the male with the female, and that they then sustain this relationship for the rest of their lives, as a couple — unlike sled dogs and caribou and men and women. And there comes a time when the occasional cobra will get killed by some over-zealous hunter, some nervous little man. And when this happens, the surviving cobra, the mate of the snake just killed, will find that man, the killer of his mate, will hunt him down even if it should take him thirty years and more, even if he should have to travel from the pale yellow dust of Punjab province to the border of Nepal or even to North America somewhere, perhaps Vancouver — he will travel there, this other cobra, somehow, even in the realm of the dream world, and he will find that man and he will kill that man, that over-zealous hunter, that nervous little man. Then, and only then, will that cobra, the lover snake, lie down and die.

Many, many years later, Dahljeet and I ceased to be friends. Something happened. Something died inside of me. I haven't seen him in many years; he and I, we've lost touch. I understand that he lives still in Vancouver, and has become even more the academic, the scholar, the thinker he was so much back then, that he teaches at one of the universities, so I've learned only recently, lecturing on the teachings of some obscure Eastern philosopher whose work relies to a great degree on the inner workings of myth and legend. I, on the other hand, now make my home in north-western Ontario, working in the field of radio broadcasting and helping as much as I can — as poet, writer, thinker after my own fashion — to revive the breathing, the singing, and the shrieking of that half-crazed little Cree clown, Weesageechak, that essential spirit many had thought was on his way to dying, to leaving forever these snow-white landscapes so precious to us all. Now that we're over thirty years of age, we've lost touch, Dahljeet and I. This is the way of things, they say, the natural course of events in the lives of friendships, of love.

But I refuse that explanation. For me, it is a pale, flimsy story, of no consequence, no fantastic substance. I hold, instead, this magazine photograph in front of me and I gaze into it and I wonder if that isn't Dahljeet there in his brilliant orange turban and his fine, dark beard. And the snake? The cobra, the lover snake, come to lay claim to his over-zealous hunter, his nervous little man. And kill him ... kill ... kill.

Dahljeet and I, we are no longer friends.

FEATURE INTERVIEW

Tomson Highway

Pulp Literature: 'The Lover Snake' *is an intimate exploration of love and loss. What is it like to encounter your words from thirty years ago? Are there any reverberations or surprises?*

TH: It was a nice surprise. Back when I wrote it, I didn't even know I could write. I never even wanted to become a writer in the first place. I just wanted to learn how to write clearly and neatly in a language which was as foreign to me as Arabic is to you, or Mandarin, or Swahili. My first dream was to be a concert pianist. And I still am, in a sense, as a side plate, when you consider the cabaret concerts I play with friends here, there, and everywhere. And a nice plate it is.

Writing? It pays the rent, so to speak, and pays it nicely. I am very happy.

PL: Language is a very particular lens through which we understand and interact with the world. Cree and Dene were your first languages, to which English, French, and Spanish were later added. How do the different languages influence the creation and execution of your various artistic pursuits?

TH: First of all, replace Spanish with Italian, please; I speak bad Spanish, but very good Italian. And add music, please, as in the language of Brahms and Chopin, a language that I speak with complete fluency. How do the different languages influence the creation, etc.? One feeds the other, and back and forth and back and forth. For instance, I always think musically, as in rhythm, form, phrasing, breathing, structure, etc. To me, each sentence is a song and thus has to sing. I think fugally; I think symphonically, in terms of form, of dynamic.

PL: Well known as you are for your award-winning plays, such as The Rez Sisters *and* Dry Lips Oughta Move to Kapuskasing, *you are also an accomplished pianist and composer. What authors and musicians do you turn to for inspiration or comfort?*

TH: For perfect form in literature, I turn to Jane Austen who, to me, is the literary equivalent of Mozart, in terms of form and structure. For musical structure, I turn to Bach, Beethoven, and, for sheer purity of lyrical line, Chopin.

PL: In The Rez Sisters *we meet Nanabush, a trickster and teacher of lessons. If he were the Bingo Master for today's world, what do you think he might want us to learn?*

TH: To learn to pray. The world has forgotten how to pray. My parents had twelve children, five of whom they lost: two as babies, one aged three, one aged seven, and one aged nine — all well before I was born. I am the eleventh and I never knew them. In fact, there was one four-year period in the forties when they lost one child a year, mostly due to the harsh living conditions of Canada's subarctic. We were all born in tents pitched in snowbanks on either one or another of the 10 000 lakes that constitute the northern ten percent of Manitoba. And you have never seen a couple — my parents — pray harder and longer, once in the morning and once at bedtime, on their knees with their elbows on the bed. And then there was Sunday. And Feast Days and on and on and on. Nothing—NOTHING!—makes one fall faster to their knees and pray harder than death. Which is what we are facing, en masse, today. Yes, it is time for the world to re-learn how to pray. And pray sincerely.

PL: *With your children's books, you speak to a whole new generation. As a 'teacher of lessons' yourself, perhaps, what do you enjoy most about sharing your stories with children? What are the unique considerations for connecting with a younger audience?*

TH: Laughter. Laughter, laughter, and yet more laughter.

PL: *What are you working on now?*

TH: Nothing in particular, just enjoying my health.

PL: *And finally, we have to ask this newest and strangest of questions: how did you spend your COVID-19 quarantine days?*

TH: In the arms of my lover of thirty-six years in our beautiful house in our beautiful cottage-country-like neighbourhood here in Gatineau, a five-minute walk from the Ottawa River where it widens out to become a lake so that you can hear its waves from our terrace on windy days (and windy nights). When not reading, he does jigsaw puzzles on the dining room table, while I sit in the living room some four feet behind him and play Brahms Intermezzi and heartbreaking country waltzes — my own compositions — at my six-foot Steinway concert grand piano. And we are very much in love.

SELECTED BIBLIOGRAPHY

The (Post) Mistress, Talonbooks, Vancouver, 2013

Ernestine Shuswap Gets Her Trout, Talonbooks, Vancouver, 2005

Aria, in *Staging Coyote's Dream Volume 1: An Anthology of First Nations Drama in English*, Playwrights Canada Press, Toronto, 2003

Fox on the Ice, HarperCollins Canada, Toronto, 2003

Rose, Talonbooks, Vancouver, 2003

'Comparing Mythologies', University of Ottawa Press, Ottawa, 2002

Dragonfly Kites, HarperCollins Canada, Toronto, 2002

Caribou Song, HarperCollins Canada, Toronto, 2001

Kiss of the Fur Queen, Doubleday Canada, Toronto, 1998

Dry Lips Oughta Move To Kapuskasing, Fifth House, Saskatoon, 1989

The Rez Sisters, Fifth House, Saskatoon, 1988

THE EXTRA: FRANKIE RAY STANDS ALONE

Mel Anastasiou

Mel Anastasiou writes the Fairmount Manor Mysteries, starring Mrs Stella Ryman; the Hertfordshire Pub Mysteries, starring Spencer Stevens; and the Monument Studios Mysteries, starring Frankie Ray and Connie Mooney. She teaches the 'Writing Success' segment of Pulp Literature Press's writing school, Quit the Day Job, and she wrote the steampunk-themed The Writer's Boon Companion: Thirty Days Towards an Extraordinary Volume and The Writer's Friend and Confidante.

The Extra:
A Monument Studios Mystery

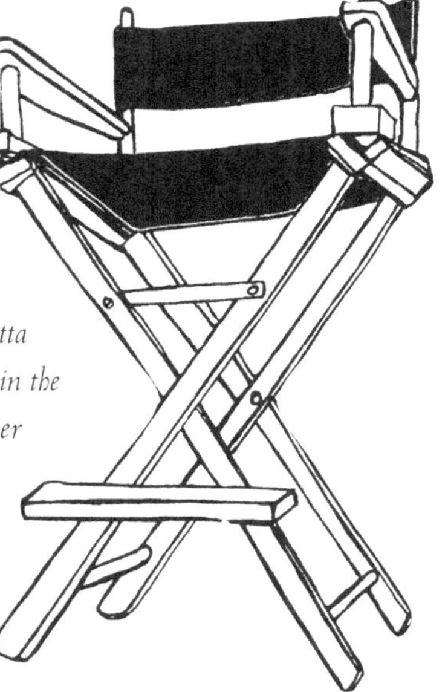

Hollywood, April 1934. Following the startling discovery of an unknown corpse buried behind her Sunset Boulevard bungalow at Paradise Gardens, Hollywood extra Frankie Ray — Vancouver schoolmarm, Hollywood hopeful, and reluctant sleuth — finds her fortunes are turning on her first day's work at Monument Studios. All the murderous powers at play among producer King Samson, loose-cannon movie star Gilbert Howard, and the stunningly ambitious superstar Marietta Valdes can't rob Frankie of her moment in the camera's eye when the director chooses her to play a scene. But the higher Frankie flies, the greater the peril, and she isn't the only one making soaring, dangerous choices. We find her on the movie set, poised for her big chance.

CHAPTER ONE

Frankie faced the director. She was distantly aware of Marietta's red dress, the movie set of a park in Paris, the enormous gleaming camera, and the crowd of staring extras. If she didn't grasp this chance at a part, even one without words, one of the other extras surely would.

She asked, "What would you like me to do?" There was something wrong with that sentence. "Sir?"

The director looked at the assistant director.

The assistant director barked, "Do what you're told."

"Do what we chose you to do." The director grinned around the cigar in his mouth. "Look sad, kid."

Frankie checked her physical position. It wouldn't do to put her hands in her pockets, so she cupped one hand inside the other to stop her fingers shaking. She guessed that amateur actors, if asked to look sad, would screw up their eyebrows and cry. Instead, Frankie did nothing but think about the body behind Villa 7A. It wasn't difficult—she hadn't stopped thinking about that poor man all morning.

The director grunted and tapped the ash from his cigar.

"I told you," Marietta Valdes said. "She is right for this scene."

"There's no screen credit in it," the assistant director told Frankie. "And same pay—as a general extra."

This was rather unfair, but she said, "Yes, sir."

"Don't talk. You have no lines." The assistant director jerked a thumb at the pedestal underneath the statue of the soldier on the horse. "Where's that damned pigeon handler?"

A cooing, bird-filled box on legs stumbled out of the crowd of extras, and the pigeon handler set the box down at the edge of the square. He opened the wire net door and shooed a small but talkative flock of pigeons toward her. She managed not to take a step back as the flock approached.

The assistant director pointed his chin at Frankie. "Sit on the pedestal, in front of the statue, pigeon girl. Feed the pigeons. And don't make it look like you're enjoying yourself."

Frankie nodded. Would they give her something with which to feed the pigeons? Birds could not be expected to act.

The director himself spoke again. "And don't make it look too easy. Don't throw it away, you know what I'm saying?"

"Yes, sir." She knew exactly what he was saying. Not everyone would, she supposed, but she did. The director wanted focus and sorrow.

She sat down among the pigeons on the grey-painted wooden pedestal by the statue's hoofs. She expected the birds to take off in a purring chaos and settle atop the soldier's hat like they did at the war memorial back home, but not a bird among the lot took wing. Although pigeons couldn't act, they apparently were trainable, because against all her experience of pigeon behaviour, they tottered around on the pavement at her feet like so many feathered wind-up toys.

A movie camera almost as big as its operator rolled on rubber wheels toward her. Frankie kept her eyes on the birds.

The pigeons must have had their wings clipped. It was a sensible way to control birds, although hard on the creatures themselves. She held out her empty hand—she was, after all, acting—and wished she really had some feed to give the poor flightless creatures. All at once she remembered the cheese sandwich Connie had given her before filming. Had she eaten it? She touched the pocket of her green and blue dress and pulled out a bit of bread. She scattered the crumbs to the pigeons. Ought she feed them dry bread instead of this fresh stuff? Well, there was nothing to do about that. And she dared not give them bits of cheese — it might make them sick.

She couldn't hear the camera. She tried not to imagine its hum as it recorded the work she was doing. She'd bet her forty remaining dollars — housed under the sofa cushions at Paradise Gardens — that thinking about the camera was almost as unprofessional as looking into its lens. Instead she focussed on the pigeons as they bustled around her, pecking at the crumbs. She felt that the scene was going quite well until a seagull swooped over the wall that separated this movie's set from the top of the gilded towers of the old *Ambition* set.

Without meaning to, she jerked her head up to watch the seagull dive at the pigeons. The director made a cutting motion to the assistant director, who called to the cameraman to stop the shot. The cameraman waved to the pigeon handler. The latter dealt with the situation by shooing the seagull away. It flew off, shrieking.

Marietta Valdes stepped up beside the director. The actress's red dress gleamed as she gestured with one pale hand. "Freddy, I know I don't have to tell *you* that with a non-speaking part, the shape and movement of the actor's body is translated into sound."

"Teach your grandmother." The director screwed his face into shapes that would terrify a dog.

Marietta leaned toward Frankie. "Movement produces sound you cannot hear, the way a person produces a shadow even on a cloudy day." She turned back to the director. "Give her another chance, will you?"

Another chance. Frankie stared. Horror gripped her. She had been certain she was acting well. To discover that she was failing was like believing she could fly, only to plummet to the ground like a dying bird.

Marietta told the director, "Shoot the scene again, Freddie."

The director glowered. "You are a damned back-seat-driving female actress, and I ought to walk right off this set. Whereupon the insurance company will take everything Monument Studios has got, right down to Samson's silk underdrawers."

Marietta Valdes smiled her goddess's smile. "Freddie, what did Gilbert Howard say to you the last time you raised the question of his insurability?"

"That damned no-show Gilbert Howard. Where the hell is he anyway?" The director raised his arms to the sky. "But hellfire, Marietta, you're right. We'll shoot the scene again. Did you hear what she said, pigeon girl?"

"Yes, sir," Frankie said.

"All acting is changing from the light to the dark, or from the dark to the light," Marietta added, looking directly at her.

"You've said enough, Marietta. Put a sock in your pretty mouth." The director pointed his cigar at Frankie. "You understand what she means? Even though you're a pigeon girl with no lines, transformation is what I'm looking for. Understand?"

Frankie was so far from understanding him that she nearly burst into tears. With a blast of certainty, she knew the role would go to Connie, as it was always meant to go. Or even to an extra she didn't know. Nature would take its course, and Frankie would return to the anonymous crowd, where she belonged. How foolish she had been, how optimistic, how blind, to think that because Gilbert Howard had started out a schoolteacher like her, that she could act, like him. She was not an actress. She was an engaged woman, here for the short term and properly one of a large group of extras. Being an extra in the movies had been enough for her an hour ago. It would have to suffice again. *Darn* it all to the deepest pit of Hades.

Then, as one holds one's nose and leaps from the highest board into a swimming pool far below, she clasped both hands before her and said, "I understand completely."

"All right. Jesus H. Christ! Shoot it again." The director pointed his cigar stub at her. "Feed the blasted pigeons, you sad little pigeon girl."

There was a sudden silence on the lot.

How lucky that she had been too sad to eat. She crumbled up more of the bread from her pocket and scattered it in front of the pigeons. She ignored the cry of the seagull, shrieking somewhere behind the dog-faced god over the wall that separated the Parisian square from the set of *Ambition*, soon to be burned. It circled back overhead, still racketing, and landed among the pigeons to peck at the crumbs in the gravel at Frankie's feet. The seagull didn't look even slightly Parisian. Its grey and white lines were a graceful reminder of the seagulls that were so much a part of her home on the coastal waters up north. Like Frankie, this bird was a west coaster, and was bound to spoil the shot.

The director threw his hat on the ground. "Cut. Dammit, do something about that bird."

The seagull took wing again. The pigeon handler fumbled in his box. Frankie supposed he must be after a net, whatever good that would do him with a high-flying seagull. She fished in her pockets for another bit of sandwich and thus she didn't see what he did. She heard it, though, a sound like a firework, or like a car backfiring—a sound similar to the echoing *crack* she'd heard the night before, under the starry sky at Paradise Gardens. But this was closer, of course, and it scattered the pigeons around the statue's base. She looked up to see the pigeon handler lower a gun to his side. The grey and white body of the seagull thudded onto the gravel at his feet. Its breast was torn into a jagged red mess.

Frankie stood up, crumbs falling from her lap. She stared at the dead bird, then sat down again, tears coursing down her face. With trembling hands, she found in her pocket a few more crumbs for the pigeons. The pigeons gobbled at them without the least regard for their dead avian colleague.

The director swore. "Luigi, get the goddam close-up."

"*Fottiti, bastardo.*" Luigi pulled the camera closer. To Frankie he said, "Little extra, the show must go on."

Frankie nodded. She knew it was true, but it didn't help. Still sobbing, she tucked her legs under her and spread her blue-and-green flowered skirt a little for the shot as the camera rolled closer. She tried not to think about the camera or the dead seagull, or the dead man at Paradise Gardens. Instead, tears streaming, she focused on the pigeons. She gave them names. *Cleo, Henry, Farthingale, Martha* . . . somehow she retained enough sense not to say the names out loud. *Isabella, Chip* . . .

Marietta Valdes called out, "*Cut.* Look about you, pigeon girl. There's more in this world than pigeons."

"Shut up, Marietta," the director bellowed. "Luigi, you don't cut unless I tell you to. Marietta's right, though, pigeon girl. Look around so we can see your sorrowful face."

Luigi remounted his camera and rose slowly to an overhead vantage.

Frankie tossed the birds her last bit of sandwich, and then pretended — *acted* — as if she had more. She held her character. She fed the pigeons, and Luigi filmed her feeding them.

"Bury your face in your hands, now, pigeon girl," the director said. "Weep but don't move. Don't move a muscle."

Go slow, kid. In Vancouver, her first stage director had told her so again and again. Now, Frankie went slow. She lowered her face into her hands. She wept for the dead seagull and for the poor soul buried in Eugene Ellery's backyard. She wept, but she didn't move her shoulders. She wept until she ran out of tears.

"Cut and print," the director said. "Money shot, that one. Not so dusty, Luigi."

"*Che cazzo,*" Luigi muttered.

"Burn it, AD. Send the pigeons and the extra crew on break."

There was a groan of pleasure from the extras, and Frankie rejoined the crowd as it headed for the square and the refreshment trolley. She wanted to shout, "*Klahowya!*" She wanted to tell her long-gone mother everything, and compose boastful missives to her father and Champ. Above all, she wanted to talk the whole scene over with Connie.

Tom, with a hoot of pleasure for her victory on the set, took Frankie under his wing. He grabbed a cup of coffee somebody handed back to them and passed it to Frankie. She tipped the cup back, thanking her stars the liquid was lukewarm and could slide straight down to her firmament.

"Where's Connie?" Frankie asked. "Did she see the take?"

"She's your best friend, isn't she? How could she miss it? Maybe afterwards she ran to the bathroom." Tom shrugged. "You want more coffee?" He walked off toward the trolley.

"Not bad for a pigeon girl," a voice said from behind her.

She turned. The director nodded his head at her. Before she could think what to say, he had joined the assistant director, who was locked in what appeared to be some kind of power struggle with the cameraman.

The director stabbed at his assistant director with his cigar. "I want you to find that dilettante Gilbert Howard and tell him the next time he doesn't show up for a scene with me, I'll have him roasted and served up for supper."

He stalked away in the direction of the further sound stages.

"Thank you, sir," Frankie told the director's receding back, although she knew he'd never hear. She'd had her moment on film. The director had searched her out personally and approved her in her first role, and perhaps her last, depending on her luck and the twisting winds of fate. Now she was an extra again. For good.

Or maybe not.

She cursed herself for a coward and raced after the director, without the slightest idea how on earth to stop him. But he stopped on his own. He dropped the stub of his last cigar into the gravel path at his feet. He fished in his pocket, pulled out a fresh cigar, bit down on one end, but didn't light it.

A massive soundstage stood open and workmen hustled by, smoking and carrying paint cans and pails full of tools.

Frankie said, "Sir? May I please ask you something?"

"Who's that?" The director frowned and produced a wet

sound from behind the cigar. "Oh, the pigeon girl. Again. Listen, are you one of those pushy, overtalented English?"

"No, sir. I'm Canadian. From Vancouver." She stopped before she told him her street number.

The director walked on, but he didn't swear at her, so she walked alongside him, ducking around the workmen, who hardly seemed to see her.

"Sir, in your next picture, are there any parts uncast? That I might be cast in? Since I was your excellent choice for pigeon girl?"

She held her breath. This man reminded her so much of her cantankerous father.

"I didn't say *excellent*." The director strode toward the building that the Queen of the Extras had pointed out to Frankie and Connie as the commissary. Frankie hesitated no more than a second before rejoining him, trotting along at his side. When he stopped without warning, Frankie did a little dance step to keep from thudding up against him.

"But, sir, you did mention I was good as the pigeon girl."

He said, "Sure I did. You were right for the pigeon girl role, but I gotta tell you: you don't have the looks to make it in this business."

"Yes, sir." As she tried to keep her chin up, Frankie had to duck around three men and a ladder. She was really going to have to develop a thick skin about all these negative comments regarding her looks — the way writers needed to develop a thick skin about having their manuscripts returned marked *boring and redundant*. Her father's collected sermons had several times been marked thus by unappreciative publishers of religious prose.

She said to the director, "But can't you see me as a not-so-pretty secretary or the friend who never finds love?"

"You're too pretty for that. But in twenty years you might make a decent character actress." The director chewed his cigar wetly.

"I see, sir." Too late, Frankie understood that she'd got the director's type wrong. He wasn't like her father, after all. He was like the principal at the school where she used to teach. They both had that particular square-shaped back and low, shiny neck. If it was no skin off his nose, a man like that didn't mind a question, respectfully phrased and appropriately punctuated. But he wouldn't give a dog he liked a bone it wanted.

So she thanked him again for the pigeon role. Then she turned and walked away.

And to be truthful, Frankie would have been an ungrateful beast not to feel pretty darned good about the morning. She was sorry nature hadn't given her the correct combination of gumption and beauty — like Connie's — with which to convince the director to cast her in a speaking part. But for now it was enough to know that she had excelled at what she'd always known in her heart would be her first step on the path to stardom in the movies: being an extra. The director had pulled her from the ranks. He had tested her without warning. And she had not been found wanting.

Furthermore, this same director, a man whose every behaviour proved that he was not given to polite white lies, had hunted her down among the other extras to tell her she'd done well. *And* he'd told her she was too pretty to play plain. She watched him as he rumbled toward a building that appeared more administrative than practical, ducking to avoid three men hefting a flower-embellished coffin. Frankie knew it for a phony, movie-set coffin — as a defrocked minister's daughter, she knew it would take six men to carry a real one — but her heart thudded and her eyes welled. She wondered what they did with the coffins after the movie. Might there not be one for the poor man buried in the backyard at Paradise Gardens? She felt an odd pivotal sensation in the area of her stomach. Without further thought, she scurried after the director and caught up with him again. "Sir——" she began.

"Listen, pigeon girl, you're becoming a pest. You're lucky I never remember an extra's face." The director glared.

"It's a blessing, I guess." Frankie swallowed. "Haven't you got *any* small role I could play?"

"When I say *no*, I mean *go to hell*." He stomped two paces off, spun on his heel, and stomped the two paces back. "Yes. I do have a part for a sad little manicurist. The actress that was to play her ran off, the devil knows where. Like Gilbert Howard, damn his eyes. The part's not much, a few lines for a very sad little girl with a very sad little life."

Frankie hardly understood what he was saying at first. She had to run the words back through the channels of her mind, weed them of her negative expectations, and listen to them again. She said, "Yes, please," then added, "sir. Thank you, sir."

She felt her face lighting up with joy and wonder. She'd never feel sad again.

The director scowled. "I said, be *sad*. I need a *sorrowful* girl. Don't get happy on me before Monday. That's when I'll test you. Two days later, we start shooting. What's your name?"

"Francesca Ray, sir." She stood up tall, schooling her features into sorrowful lines——but not too sorrowful. She was not a ham. She was an actress. An actress who, this coming Monday, would win a role in a moving picture. An actress who in two days would have lines.

An actress.

The director said, "I'll never remember your face or your name. It's the way I am, and I like it. If you tell me you're the pigeon girl, then you can test. Get it?"

"Got it." It took all her acting talent and discipline not to burst into joyous song right in front of the director. As an actress with lines, Frankie would have her name at the end of the movie. She would roll with the credits: *Sad Little Manicurist … Francesca Ray.* Frankie was so happy, she could have hugged the director all the way around his long canvas coat, and what a mistake that would be. Her eyes widened, and she wished above all things that the director would go away before she simply … popped.

He called over his shoulder, "Show up at 5 a.m. two days from now and see casting. And, pigeon girl …"

"Yes, sir?"

"You're a manicurist. A sad one. So you're going to have to dye your hair blonde."

Her heart raced. "Yes, sir."

"*Platinum.*"

"I will, sir," she called to the director's square back as he slammed through the door into the commissary.

Frankie walked back along the path to the extras' gravel yard, taking in the smell of cigarette ends and paper cups of coffee like heaven's aroma. The dead body in the backyard at Paradise Gardens still haunted her, but for now those white fingers couldn't touch her.

Alone among the smoking, sipping, milling extras, she held her great new chance close to her. In that moment, she understood how it would be to be Loretta Desirée, the Queen of the Extras, and to want to give her boys and girls all the good luck a day could possibly bring them. She wanted to hug every single extra to her breast, individually and in a group, and offer them all roles with their coffee. She'd love to lead them all in a chorus of *"Hi de Hi de Ho."* And then she would take the whole lot for a ride in the Model A, straight down the middle of Sunset Boulevard with all the kids hanging out the windows. She wanted to call out to the sellers of Maps of the Stars, "Print up a new map, and write our names around the edges in gold type." But most of all, she was dying to tell Connie.

She looked toward the crowd at the coffee trolley, and over into the shadows by the toilet block, but Connie was nowhere in sight.

"Hey, Pigeon Frankie." Tom, leaning against the wall with his skirt bunched up behind him, upraised his coffee to her.

She asked him where she might find Connie, but he shook his head. "She might have gone to the beach with Doris in the truck. There's a loose board in the fence. Some of the less motivated extras use it to get out of the studio, go swimming, and creep back in without losing their day's pay."

"Connie would never sneak away to the beach. Even if the others did." Frankie frowned and took one of the remaining tomato sandwiches from the trolley. "Connie's too much of a professional to skip out on the day. I'll try the WC again."

But there was no sign of Connie at sink or in stall. Frankie, chewing on her soggy sandwich, got directions to the loose board in the studio wall and slipped through it onto the street. A limousine drove past at high speed toward Sunset Boulevard, its driver in an outside seat hanging onto his cap by its brim. Two policemen in white and blue paid no attention to the speeding car, but looked her up and down before rounding the corner. Her afternoon shadow moved blackly against the high, grey studio walls. She saw no sign of Connie.

Frankie stood on the sidewalk in the sunshine. She swallowed her last bit of tomato. If she were Connie, where would she be? When they were children, if Connie wanted to escape, she would hide under the weeping willow down by the reserve land. But that was when she was in a fury because she hadn't gotten her way. Whenever Connie got into a temper, Frankie was always the one to end up in some kind of trouble.

And now, Frankie had left the movie set on her first day on the job. Without permission. She must make her way back to the set before anybody in authority noticed she was gone. She must not spoil her chances. Not for anything.

A big sedan drove by. Long and silent, it was at a guess twice the size of the Model A, and probably four times the price. It purred past her, and for a moment, Frankie envied the passenger sitting in what must be a luxurious back seat. As the sedan sped up, the passenger turned to look out. Connie stared back at Frankie through the rear window.

Frankie ran after the sedan, but it rounded the corner and passed out of sight.

Chapter Two

The black sedan's license plate read *3T 59 90*. Frankie had no way to write it down, but she did her best to commit the numbers to memory. Feeling every second as a yard or more that Connie was travelling in who-knew-what perilous situation,

Frankie broke into a run along the sidewalk that bordered the high studio walls. *3T 59 90.*

She saw with a start that the Model A was not empty. A blonde woman sat in the passenger seat. Frankie yanked open the driver's door and flung herself behind the wheel.

"Either get out, or you're going for a ride."

"Okay, honey." The blonde blinked at her sleepily, and in the seconds that it took Frankie to push the key into the Model A's starter and turn it, she recognized Billie Starr, the girl from the Spanish-style mansion. Billie Starr, from the brothel. The girl who had tried to walk under the wheels of the Model A the day before.

This afternoon, Billie was dressed in a pair of men's heliotrope-striped pyjamas. She said, "I knew I remembered your car from yesterday, when you almost hit me."

"We didn't. You walked into us."

"Well, no hard feelings," Billie said. "I found you anyhow. I was about to invite you to our house tonight. The other girls and I are going to sit upstairs and watch them burn the set of *Ambition*. But a ride is always nice. Where are we going?"

"Oh, for heaven's sake. Hang on." Frankie put the car into gear.

"Hurrah," Billie said.

"Look here, Billie. You're my eyes. Watch for a black sedan, license plate *3T 59 90*. When you see it, stand up and holler out, *Stop*."

"Okay." Billie folded her hands in her heliotrope-striped lap. "I'm a smidgen drunk, though."

"Wonderful. Just look for *3T 59 90*, will you?" Frankie signalled with her left hand, and a van with a cockroach painted on the side almost clipped the front left bumper of the Model A.

"You have to check the traffic before you pull out," Billie explained.

Frankie gritted her teeth and entered traffic, narrowly missing a brightly painted truck full of handsome young Mexicans sitting on crates of oranges in the truck bed. One of the young men grinned and lobbed a couple of oranges at them. Billie reached up both hands like a lifelong outfielder and missed them both. The fruit splatted down onto the road behind the Model A.

Frankie leaned over the wheel and steered east along Sunset Boulevard. "Is that a black sedan up ahead?"

"Nope. Brown. Say! I know this road. This is how you drive to Mexico."

"Lord, I'll never find Connie in Mexico." Frankie drove faster along Sunset Boulevard. Without thinking, she said, "Today, I won an audition for a role in Samson's new film, *The Emperor of New York.*"

"I knew it! Congratulations." Billie clapped her hands together like a little kid. Then she reached down, pulled up from the floor a bottle of something brownish, unscrewed the top, and raised the bottle in salute.

"Thanks," Frankie said. "I don't really know how to behave like a movie actress, but I guess I'll learn. And . . ." She felt her excitement mount and had to remind herself to watch for black vehicles. "And I have to become a platinum blonde."

"Blonde is best. Yikes!" One hand on the windshield, Billie half stood in the passenger seat. "Stop!"

"Do you see the sedan? Where is it, Billie? Hang on." Frankie pulled over with a juddering groan to the wrong side of the street. With a cough, the Model A rolled in beside a drugstore, one back wheel up on the sidewalk, which saved her having to switch it off. She shielded her eyes with one hand and peered out from the shadow of the drugstore's green-striped awning, up and down the road of shops. It was difficult to see straight with so many stripes — on the awnings, Billie's pyjamas, and in the shadows of the swaying palms that cut diagonally across cars, people, and even the road itself. "Where's that black car?"

"I didn't see your black car." Billie opened the car door. "I stopped you because I need to go into this drugstore for a minute."

Frankie reached out too late to stop Billie as she stepped out of the car into the path of an oncoming laundry truck. The driver sounded his horn and Billie blew him a raspberry. Her pyjama top lifted slightly with the wind as she crossed in front of the Model A and entered the shadows under the green-striped drugstore awning.

Frankie opened the car door to follow Billie into the drugstore, but before she could step down, Billie re-emerged, a pair of men's dark glasses on her pretty nose and another pair in her hand, along with a small green bottle. Given the lack of any sort of money-carrying pocket in those pyjamas, or indeed anything else except Billie herself, Frankie had to ask, "Did you pay for those things?"

"Think I'm a chump?" Billie climbed back into the Model A. "Better drive fast, Frankie. Here, put these on. They're all the rage now."

Billie settled the second pair of men's sunglasses on Frankie's nose as an angry-looking woman bustled through the drugstore door into the shade of the awning. Would the woman listen and understand, or would she call the police and have both Billie and Frankie arrested? With a squeal of conscience, Frankie pulled back out onto the road and tried not to remember Sunday school lessons regarding honesty with tradesmen.

She snatched the dark glasses from her nose and hid them in her skirt pocket.

Billie tucked the little bottle into Frankie's other pocket. "That's peroxide, is what that is. We'll have you dyed as platinum as Jean Harlow in no time. Maybe I'll go from blonde to platinum, too."

Billie opened the glove box and pulled out a pack of Lucky Strike cigarettes that she must have stashed there. With a start, Frankie remembered King Samson's gun, and thanked her stars that it was no longer in the glove box for Billie to fool around with. She reminded herself to look for the gun in the bushes between Paradise Gardens and the Garden of Allah. That's where she had dropped it while she, Tom, and Connie had watched Gilbert Howard with his lover, the golden swimmer.

Billie was uncorking her bottle. "Say, chum, want a drink?"

"Not now, thank you, Billie." Frankie steered straight ahead.

Billie held out the pack of cigarettes. "Here you go, Frankie."

"I don't smoke, thanks."

"No, sweetie. Your friend Connie left the pack for you."

Frankie started. "*Connie* did?" She took the pack from Billie. It was empty.

"You know — Connie. That red-headed girl you were with yesterday."

"Yes. I do know Connie." Frankie breathed into her diaphragm to calm down, the way they taught you in acting class. "*When* did she give you this cigarette pack?"

"Couple minutes before you ran up to the car." Billie took another swig from the bottle. "She tossed it to me before she got into a black car. She said you'd understand."

These cigarettes must be a message from Connie, in their secret code. Frankie could almost hear Connie sing out, *Hey, Frankie, what do you want in a cigarette?*

Frankie tried the question aloud as she drove along Sunset Boulevard. "*What do I want in a cigarette?*"

"If you don't know, sister, I can't tell you." Billie took another swig. In her blonde glory, in her pyjamas, she looked like a movie star on the lam.

"This cigarette pack is a coded message," Frankie said. "Connie and I always talk in code." However, their excellent private code was much easier to understand when Frankie was able to ask Connie face-to-face exactly what a coded message meant.

Billie peered at the pack. She read out loud, "*Lucky Strike* cigarettes. Maybe Connie struck it lucky?"

"Yes." Frankie nodded sharply. "Or cigarettes might mean a *smokescreen*—but hiding what? And why drive away like that, right after I was chosen to be pigeon girl and had wangled an audition ..." She trailed off.

"Maybe she feels funny about your good fortune?" Billie shot Frankie a sideways glance. "A teeny bit green about the gills with envy?"

Possibly. But Frankie answered, "Never."

"Well, then." Billie took another drink. "It stands to reason that if Connie was handing me cigarette packages, she certainly wasn't being strong-armed into that shiny sedan."

Frankie gripped the steering wheel and logicked furiously in and out of a dozen different dead-end directions. At last she said, "I think you are right. I think Connie had some good luck. But what?"

"Maybe she got a ride home," Billie said.

Frankie took her eyes off the road to stare at Billie. *Out of the mouths of babes and drunkards.* "You're a genius, Billie. While I was talking to the director, Connie would have looked for me, and when she couldn't find me, I'll bet she accepted a ride."

Billie sucked her lip and nodded. "A ride home, like the one I wish somebody would give me. I'm sick of that mansion full of prostitutes."

"Sure as shooting. You're coming home with me, Billie Starr," Frankie said. Grinding the car into gear, she made a great bleating U-turn back through the traffic. Then she headed down Sunset Boulevard toward Monument Studios. "Connie and I can crowd together to make room for three at Villa 7B."

"I'll dye your hair platinum," Billie said happily.

"You'll have to stop drinking," Frankie told her.

"I drink because I'm so unhappy." Billie's smile was sunny. "I'll stop when I'm a star in the movies. I knew you'd be good luck for me the minute you picked me up from the sidewalk yesterday. And I'm going to be good luck for you, too. Because I've got a friend who can help us all."

"Who?" Frankie drove past two straw-hatted movie-star map sellers touting their wares in front of the golden angels of Monument Studios. On the other side of the road, the Spanish-style mansion Billie had so recently left stretched out amid its flowered gardens. A tan-and-red roadster rumbled out from the studio drive. Frankie wavered at the wheel, and, coming up behind, the roadster honked like a goose.

"Who can help us?"

"What?" Billie asked. "Who do you mean?"

"You said you have a friend who can help you, me, and Connie in the movies."

"Yes."

"Who?"

"Guess," Billie answered.

Bearing up behind them, the blonde at the wheel of the tan-and-red roadster honked at them again.

"Ye gods!" Frankie peered into the rear-view. Blanche Carver, the Hollywood columnist, sat at the wheel, and beside her in the passenger seat sat Leo. "Would you look at who's behind us?"

"Who?"

"Guess."

Billie made a squeaking noise and stood up backward in her seat, leaning on the passenger backrest. "I don't need you anymore," she shouted at the roadster.

"Sit down, Billie." Frankie pulled at Billie's pyjama hem, but Billie paid no attention. While Leo half-rose to his feet in his mother's sports car, Billie shouted, "I've got somebody who can really help me now!"

"If you fall out of the car, you'll be bashed to bits," Frankie said.

Billie called out to Leo, "I'm friends with Gilbert Howard. A great big famous movie star! So there!" She threw herself back down into the seat and then pushed with her own foot upon Frankie's foot over the gas pedal. Frankie felt the Model A lurch forward. She held on hard to the steering wheel, all the while pushing at Billie's foot to regain control of the accelerator. In this unsatisfactory manner, they pulled up to Paradise Gardens, where Frankie hauled up on the hand brake and landed them on the gravel verge.

Billie stared up through the orange branches at the wooden sign that read *Paradise Gardens*. "Didn't I used to live here?"

"Did you?" Frankie couldn't imagine anybody leaving this place if they didn't have to. Certainly not for a brothel. She asked, "Billie, were you the girl who broke Leo's heart?"

"Leo doesn't have a heart."

"He seems like a nice enough fellow to me."

Billie made a scornful face, and Frankie gave up the sales job.

The extras ought to be back soon, but in the meantime Paradise Gardens seemed to be abandoned by all except for the birds and, as it turned out, the blonde in Villa 12A.

Billie called out to 12A's open window, "Hey in there, do you wanna buy a duck?"

"Get a robe, pyjama dame." All they saw of the blonde in 12A was one white arm reaching out from the shadowy interior to slam the window shut.

"You know, you and Connie are going to get along fine." Frankie smiled at the thought. *Almost home, now.*

Frankie glanced at Billie, who — even in men's sunglasses — looked very young, balancing in her bare feet along a row of rocks that edged the yard of Villa 11B, and hitching up her pyjama bottoms with one hand. Billie was a waif and a guttersnipe. She was Oliver Twist, and Frankie and Connie would be the wise and kindly grandfather who saved her. Connie was probably home in Villa 7B by now. She might even have had time to stop by the market for milk and butter and other necessary supplies. Even now Connie was likely to be cooking her patented creamed tuna on toast, the recipe for which she'd received an *A* in high school home economics, because she added a pinch of pickle relish in the final five minutes of cooking. Frankie imagined Tom leaning in at their window, all of them laughing, eating creamed tuna, and learning to juggle oranges off their own tree out in the backyard.

The backyard. Frankie recalled almost for the first time in an hour the unknown body that was buried there.

She said, "Listen, Billie. We'll choose you a new screen name, and you'll begin your career at the movies all over again."

"Start all over again?" Billie asked. "That sounds terrible."

"You can start at the bottom, as an extra like I did, and —" She heard Billie's snort of disbelief. She stopped the girl in the pathway and looked her straight in her dark glasses. "And then you can learn as you go. Maybe you are the world's best actress, Billie, and maybe so am I. But if I'm honest with myself, I know I'm not yet ready for a *starring* role. Today, I got a chance at a small part, and that might lead to a bigger part. It'll happen to you too. I know it. You got off to a bad beginning, you maybe listened to the wrong person." She wondered who had been the one to suggest working in the brothel across from Monument Studios.

"*Hi de Hi de Hi de Hi*, I've got Gilbert Howard to help me," Billie sang as she walked down the little path to Villa 7B. "Maybe Howie will help you, too. *Ho de Ho de Ho de Ho . . .*"

Frankie nipped past her. With a dramatic gesture of welcome, she opened the door to Villa 7B.

Billie walked by her, still singing. Once inside the living room, however, she stopped mid-stanza. She made a strange little sound and stood still.

Frankie joined her. She left the door open at their backs to let in the warm evening air. The bathroom and bedroom doors stood open as well. She saw no sign of Connie. Disappointment struck her, followed closely by the realization that she and Billie were not alone.

Before them on the sofa, propped up, sat Gilbert Howard. He looked as if he'd been waiting for them for quite a while, in patient solitude.

As she looked at him more closely, Frankie noted that, for once, the movie star was fully clothed below the waist.

She saw that the fingers of one hand were curved around an orange.

And she saw that Gilbert Howard, star of the silver screen, was dead.

Chapter Three

The young woman buttoned her shirt up to her neck. She checked the clock beside her bed again. The long afternoon was at last wearing on toward evening.

What would they think when they saw the orange clasped in Gilbert's dead hand? When she'd placed it there, it had seemed an almost random addition to the scene she had set, but now she saw that it might also be interpreted as a symbol of the bounty of Gilbert Howard's spirit.

And at a second, secret level, the orange was a reference to the way his hand would touch her cheek when they were together.

How lucky she was that they'd had those few hours the night before. She'd had him almost to herself, curled up warmly in his arms before her swim. She sighed as she remembered diving into the pool, and how the water skimmed along the surface of her body. It was a sensation at once intimate and impersonal.

Swimming naked was nothing a decent woman in her hometown would contemplate, even for a moment. But Gilbert had taught her not to care who saw her. He said, "The best way to keep your secrets, my darling, is to reveal them to an uncaring world."

She would never have him to herself again.

But then, except for a few sweet hours now and again, she never had.

CHAPTER FOUR

Frankie put out a hand to the bungalow wall to steady herself. She felt as if she were two people, one who trusted her own eyes, and a second Frankie who, even with the movie star's corpse seated here in front of her on her own rented sofa, couldn't believe Gilbert Howard was really dead. How was her brain supposed to reconcile this cold, pale figure with the vibrant man he'd been the night before, reciting Webster to the blue California sky as dusk fell and a naked, golden girl leapt from his arms into the water beside him? She remembered how the spray from the girl's dive into the pool had caught the light like diamonds suspended by invisible threads, like movie magic.

Right now, around the country—no, around the world—there were hundreds of marquees with Gilbert Howard's name written on them. And only she and Billie knew that his movies and this empty body were all that remained of him. No matter that she'd only met him twice, it was plain to Frankie that the world couldn't go on without him. At least it wouldn't carry on in the same way, any more than if all the peacocks in existence spread their tails and died.

"Billie, we have to tell somebody right now."

"Not yet." Billie's tears slipped out from under her dark glasses and crept down her cheeks to the neck of her men's pyjamas. She knelt at the actor's side. She reached out and touched the orange he was holding and then the hand that held it. Gently she stroked the straight black line of his right eyebrow, and his left.

"Say something."

"He can't." But of course, Billie wasn't speaking to Gilbert Howard. She was asking Frankie to say something. Something appropriate.

But Frankie could think of nothing to say. She remembered the churchyard taunts: *Shoemakers' children go barefoot, ministers' children go bad.* She knew so many quotations—from the Bible, from Shakespeare, from Shelley. But all she remembered now were Webster's words, as Gilbert Howard had recited them beside a shining pool wherein an unnamed blonde girl splashed naked the night before: *"What would it pleasure me to have my throat cut with diamonds . . . to be shot with pearls?"* It was almost as if, by declaiming Webster, Gilbert Howard had presaged his own death.

Billie cocked her pretty head to one side, apparently thinking hard. At last she said, *"Now cracks a noble heart."*

Frankie remembered the next bit: *"Goodnight, sweet prince."*

"Yes! *Goodnight. And flights of angels sing thee to thy rest.* What will I do without you, Howie? How can I manage without your help?" Billie bent and kissed the corpse's pale cheek.

Frankie spoke past the lump in her throat. "I didn't realize you knew him so well. Did he have heart trouble?"

"Heart trouble? Howie?" Billie put her hand over her mouth, as if to stifle an ill-timed laugh. "Of course, we know who killed him."

Killed him? How could Billie say such a thing? And at such a moment? With sudden comprehension, Frankie remembered that Billie must still be drunk.

"Nobody killed him, Billie." The breeze at her back reminded her of the greater world outside Villa 7B, where this news had not yet travelled. "Even though he was a movie star, he … died. The way everybody dies, in the end. Do you see?"

Billie looked over her shoulder. Without another word, she got to her feet and slipped out of Frankie's living room by the back door. Her shadow flitted away into the darkness in the direction of the Garden of Allah bungalows.

The sound of an indrawn breath was all the warning Frankie got before Blanche Carver stepped into the room.

The columnist said, "A woman called my office. She didn't leave her name. Said Gilbert Howard had missed today's shoot at the studios and was up to something … *gossip-worthy* in Paradise Gardens …"

Frankie could think of nothing to say. She clasped her hands together and waited for the columnist to digest the truth of the scene laid out in front of her.

Blanche took two steps past Frankie toward the sofa where Gilbert Howard's body lay.

"Oh, God," Blanche said. "Howie, you *can't* be dead."

"Howie? Dead? What's happened?" Leo appeared out of the shadows outside the door. He moved toward his mother and wrapped his good arm around her. Over Blanche's shoulder, he said to Frankie, "I can't believe the old fellow's dead. He and my mother went back a long way. And on your sofa?"

Blanche lifted her head. Tears had coloured her pale cheeks pink. "This is impossible. We are old friends. We came to

Hollywood together—Howie, Loretta, and me. Have you called the studio?"

Frankie managed a tiny, negative movement of her head. Then, without warning, and without reason, her silence ended. Involuntarily, as if she had become a puppet through whom somebody else was speaking, words began to flow out of her mouth, quietly at first, and then more loudly.

"You mean, have I called the police? No, I don't have a phone, and I should have run to find one, it would have been the right thing, but we've just—*I've* just—found him, and I'm so sad and so *stupid* to do nothing to help, but the thing is that I've never—" Frankie clapped her hands across her own mouth to halt the flow.

She had been about to say that she'd never seen a dead body before in her life, but that would not be true. Her father had presided at funerals. And she'd seen that other corpse this very morning, buried out in the backyard between Eugene Ellery's bungalow and her own, hers and Connie's. That made two dead bodies in the course of one long, blue, Californian day.

Blanche stood up straight and wiped at the tears on her cheeks. "Leo, Loretta has a telephone. Call the studio."

"I'll go and tell the Queen, then, and telephone from there." Leo's voice sounded rough. Holding a hand to his shoulder where Gilbert Howard had shot him a few days before, he hurried away.

His mother sat down at the kitchen table where, that morning, Frankie and Connie had shared a light-hearted breakfast of burned toast and tea. Blanche picked up her pen and opened the notebook to a clean page. "Gilbert Howard is dead, rest his lovely soul. The rest of the world will make up lies and fairy tales around him. But I want to get this story right. In Howie's honour. Is this your home?"

"Mine and …" Frankie stopped as the woman began to write. "Yes. Mine and Connie's."

"That young redhead I met with Leo outside Monument Studios?" The columnist's eyes darted around the place to the plaid curtains, the little kitchen. She looked hardest at the orange, which had fallen from Howard's hand when Billie had touched him.

Frankie burst out, "It's terrible enough that he's dead. But he shouldn't have died *here.* Not in this little place, on that old plaid sofa. He was too grand for that."

The columnist looked narrowly at her. "What an odd thing for you to say."

Frankie wanted to ask, *What is so odd about speaking an obvious truth?* But outside, doors to other bungalows began to bang open and slam shut. Voices — young voices — were raised, calling out to one another, rising and falling in urgent interrogative tones. The news of Howard's death must have travelled to the kids who lived at Paradise Gardens, via Leo and Loretta Desirée, Queen of the Extras.

The Queen's kids began to pour into the small room, overflowing in their numbers out the front door and onto the path leading to the patio where, the evening before, they had danced around the fountain. A buzz of distressed voices swelled in Villa 7B's little living room. The press of bodies crushed Frankie against the wall nearest the bedroom. She felt invisible. She was glad to be so.

The crowd of kids craned and stared at Gilbert Howard's body on the sofa. Tom shouldered through the crowd, his voice rising above the agitated buzz in the room, asking what had happened, and then falling silent as he saw Howard's corpse.

Eugene Ellery was among the last to make his way through the crush of young people, and when she caught sight of him, Frankie felt a relief so strong that it was almost like having her father there.

The volume and pitch of the chatter rose. Leo returned, supporting a very pale Queen at his side. Blanche Carver laid a protective hand across the Queen's shoulder and helped her to her seat. She said, "Loretta here needs something hard to drink."

"There's no drink in the world hard enough to help with this." Tom headed for the door. "But I'll get some of the Queen's own store for her."

"What happened to Howie?" This from the girl nearest Gilbert Howard's body. Frankie didn't know her name, but she remembered her as one of today's extras. "How can he be dead?"

At Tom's side, Doris made a stricken noise. "Howie looks like he's sitting waiting for somebody."

"Where's that girl who lives here? The one I was talking to before?" Blanche asked. "Francesca. She found Gilbert's body."

There was a stirring in the crowd, and Frankie felt the mass of the Queen's kids turn to look at her.

She gazed from one questioning face to another. "I found him dead. But last night I saw him alive." It was hard, but these were her neighbours, and they had a right to know everything. She swallowed once, twice, thrice, and continued. "Larger than life! He was reciting Webster. *To have my throat cut by diamonds,* he said. *To be smothered by cassia* ... But he wasn't cut. He wasn't smothered. He's just dead."

"'Just dead?' I'm sure you can think of something better than that. Let's get this right for tomorrow's edition, all you mugs."

Blanche addressed the group of young people standing about Villa 7B's living room. "It's clear to me, as it must be to all of you, that Howie was waiting for his girlfriend, Francesca, here —"

At this outrageous inaccuracy, Frankie found her tongue. "I'm not his girlfriend. I hardly knew him."

Frankie felt an arm slip around her shoulder. Tom had reached her. She shot him a grateful look, and then focussed her attention back on the columnist.

Blanche said, "Or was he waiting for that red-headed friend of yours? Maybe so. Maybe it was even love at last for poor old Howie. Heaven knows enough of us girls tried to make him happy."

There was a moment of feminine agreement in the room. Doris asked, "You, too, Miss Carver?"

"Didn't everybody, at one time or another?" Blanche looked blank for a moment. Then she appeared to pull herself together. "Never mind. While he was waiting for Frankie here, Gilbert Howard slipped away. Dreaming of his new love, perhaps?"

Frankie cleared her throat and tried again. "Look, Miss Carver, even *if* I had been involved with Gilbert Howard, which I was not, I'm telling you that you've got the *wrong story.*"

"I agree." Eugene joined Tom at Frankie's side.

Blanche Carver said, "Let me get the facts right, Francesca. Step forward and clear this matter up: Was it you, or your friend Connie, who was Gilbert Howard's final lover?"

"Neither one of us," Frankie said, hanging back. "And you should be writing your story about how he was such a great *actor.* That's the important part."

"Yes," Eugene said, as the Queen's kids made noises of agreement. "He must be honoured —"

"Quiet! He was my friend. So don't worry your sad little hearts," the columnist said. "I'm determined to get the story right. Everybody who reads about his death will be comforted to know that Gilbert Howard, adored by millions, fell in love at last. I think that's wonderful. I think it's *beautiful*. Tell us how you met him, before the cops get here. We're all behind you. Aren't we, kids?"

Frankie had to struggle to keep from shouting at the woman. "Miss Carver, you should be writing about Gilbert Howard's talent, not about who his last girlfriend was. Write about how the planet may still turn, but the world won't be the same now that he's gone."

Eugene squeezed Frankie's hand, and on her other side Tom tightened his arm around Frankie's shoulder. The rest of the kids made it clear by word and posture that they were behind Frankie one hundred percent.

On the far side of the room, Doris looked out the window by the front door. She called out, "Jiggers, here come the cops!"

The crowd nearest the door parted to let a pair of policemen through. One was tall and the other handsome. The two of them approached Gilbert Howard with difficulty through the crush.

"Is it really Gilbert Howard? It is, and no mistake." The tall policeman pouched his lower lip.

The handsome policeman addressed Blanche Carver. "We've called the precinct captain. He'll send the detectives."

"But we will begin without them." The tall policeman gazed down upon the crowd in the little room. He asked, "Who here knows how Gilbert Howard died?"

The Queen of the Extras had not spoken for some time, but now she set her glass down on the table and rose to her feet.

"Everybody knows. You only have to look at poor Howie, sitting up on the sofa as if he were alive. Anybody can see he … slipped away from life."

Blanche Carver put an arm around the Queen. "Loretta has hit it on the button there. A natural death. You can see that this dear man died happy, and free of pain."

The second policeman bent over the body. He pulled Howard's jacket aside, revealing a blossom of red so dark it was almost black.

Frankie stared at the bullet wound.

She tottered and felt Eugene's supporting hand at her side. Gilbert Howard had not simply fallen dead of natural causes. Somebody had shot him.

"*Murder.*" Blanche Carver stood up.

In Villa 7B's little living room, a sort of electricity arose and travelled through the crowd, like a wordless rumour that grew in strength and conviction as it spread.

$\mathcal{C}$HAPTER FIVE

In memory, Frankie heard Gilbert Howard's voice again: *What would it pleasure me … to be shot with pearls?* Gilbert Howard had not died a natural death at all. It may not have been pearls, but he certainly was shot.

Despite the draft from the open back door behind her, the crowd in the little living room of Villa 7B was so dense Frankie found it difficult to breathe.

We all know who killed him, don't we?

Frankie had no idea whom Billie might have meant. How could anybody, no matter how black of heart and murderous, kill such a talented man? That person had to be punished. She would very much like to be a part of the machinery of the law. She wanted to see Gilbert Howard's murderer tried and sentenced. And one early morning, to the sound of convicts tapping their metal cups against the bars of their cells, she would happily witness the killer's long walk to the electric chair.

With a gaze fully as judgmental as Frankie's thoughts, the second policeman stared from face to face in the crowded living room. He asked, "Which of you found the body?"

Frankie felt Eugene's nudge. She freed herself of Tom and Eugene's support and stepped forward. "I did."

"Your name, miss?"

Frankie gave it, along with the details of finding the body. It was all perfectly true but for a lie of omission: she couldn't give Billie's address without getting her in trouble with the law for prostitution. So, she decided not to mention Billie at all. It would not, in any case, make a difference to the investigation.

"How long ago did you find the body?" The tall policeman asked.

Frankie swallowed hard at the memory. "About twenty minutes ago."

"Were the lights on in the room when you found Mr Howard?"

"No."

"Was Mr Howard's body as we see him now?"

"Yes."

"Exactly as he is now?"

"Yes."

"You didn't touch him or move him in any way?"

Frankie mumbled, "I didn't touch him. It wouldn't be respectful."

Eugene squeezed her arm. She looked gratefully at him, and then back at the policemen.

"Did you find a gun in the room?"

"No."

"No weapon at all, in the house or around it?"

"Nowhere." Frankie was glad beyond all reason that she had dropped King Samson's gun out in the bushes the night before and didn't have to explain why she had it. "No gun at all."

He licked his pencil and jotted down a note.

"Do you own a gun, Miss Ray?"

"No," Frankie stated truly. "I have never owned a gun."

"Did you know the victim, Mr Gilbert Howard, well?" the tall policeman asked. The handsome one, now apparently busy catching up on his notes, looked up as his colleague asked the question.

Blanche Carver set her notebook down. "Frankie was his lover. You don't need to wait for plainclothesmen to tell you the implications, do I?"

"I was *not* his lover," Frankie said. The sounds came out in mumbles, most unlike her usual clear tones. It was like trying to speak in a dream — every word cost her an enormous amount of energy. "He was barely an acquaintance."

The tall policeman walked over to the body. "So you say. But others say you were known to be romantically connected to the victim, and he was found in your home."

"Yes." Frankie wasn't sure she said it aloud, so she said yes again. "But only to the first part. The only times he talked to me——"

"Save the finer points for the detectives, sister. Gilbert Howard's been dead awhile, from the look of him. Our job is to ask for your movements throughout the day."

"My movements?" Frankie stared.

Tom took her elbow again. "Frankie was at the studio today. We all saw her."

"I was," Frankie said. With difficulty, she drew in a breath of thick air. "But I'd never —"

"Yes indeed. Why would she kill him?" Blanche Carver's tone was icy. She took up her pen and thumbed a new page over in her notebook. "Motive's the thing, wouldn't you say, gentlemen?"

As the columnist spoke, Frankie experienced a sensation of . . . slowness, in addition to her growing breathlessness. Everything in the room seemed to have slowed to half speed while she attempted to follow the turn the conversation had taken. A murmur animated the Paradise Gardens residents around her, a susurrus that sounded almost wary — possibly even unfriendly.

"Love. Jealousy." The tall policeman sucked his lower lip. "Did you love him, er, Frankie?"

"*No.*" She clasped her hands together. "Yes. But the way everyone loved him. As a great actor."

"I begin to see the truth of it now," Blanche Carver said, and crossed something out in her journalist's notebook.

Frankie's fingers went cold at the tips. She had never felt such a sensation before in her life.

"Was it you who phoned my office to say that something had happened to Gilbert?" Blanche Carver touched the point of her pen to the tip of her index finger. She studied the small dot it made on her skin. She asked, "Did you kill him, Frankie?"

For a moment, Frankie felt nothing at all, and then in the centre of her field of vision she saw lights swirl against a background of darkness, as if every star in the firmament had extinguished itself between her last breath and this one.

The crowded bungalow living room came back into focus. She looked from the columnist to the police, and from the extras to their Queen. Connie was gone, and Billie had run away. Her neighbours — Tom and Doris and Eugene, as well as the rest of the extras — had fallen silent. In the middle of this crowded room, Frankie was stranded as surely as if she stood on the shore of a desert isle crowded with savage beasts and encircled by sharks, with no help in sight.

Frankie glanced behind her at the open door that led out to the backyard, through the bushes, and into the Garden of Allah. But only fools tried to outwit the law. You stood your ground and let justice take its course. She didn't even need the hundred radio dramas and cinematic lessons every listener and moviegoer heard and saw every week of their life. Simple common sense, as well as her fairly good education in citizenship and history, told her that an innocent person need never fear the arm of the law. Guilty persons ran away.

Then, close to her ear: *"Don't answer."*

Frankie met Eugene Ellery's calm grey gaze.

A murmur rose in the little room. Somebody called out, "There are more coppers on the way."

Another voice added, "No more of you Keystone fellows. Plain clothes!"

"Tie a tin can to the comments, you people. It's about time we cleared the room." The two policemen conferred quietly. The handsome one jangled something in the hip pocket of his uniform.

The tall policeman faced Blanche. "Our colleagues will think it's interesting that the suspect says she loved him, and yet she isn't crying."

"You saw that, did you? She seems more disturbed than sad." Blanche touched her pencil to her lower lip. "About time you fellows noticed. I'd almost given up on the perspicacity of lawmen."

So fogged was Frankie by the unreality of the proceedings that at first she hardly noticed that her neighbours at Paradise Gardens were moving to stand close to her. Casually, still chatting, the young people shifted to form a protective wall around her in the little room. In that moment the community of extras at Paradise Gardens stopped being acquaintances and became friends. She read in their expressions belief in her innocence and fear for her safety. They quietly edged her toward the back door.

It stood ajar. Eugene Ellery touched her shoulder and made a small gesture with his head. He whispered, "Out the back door with you. Quick as a wink."

Frankie hesitated. It was so difficult to think, to reason things through. Guilty persons ran away. However, despite everything she'd always believed, there was at this moment more comfort in the extras' concern, and in Eugene's calm and trustworthy gaze, than in the faceless, long-armed law represented by those two policemen.

The Queen's extras had entirely encircled her. Knees weak, dangerously near falling, Frankie found herself manoeuvred out the back door of Villa 7B.

Eugene followed her out, took hold of her arm, pulled her inside the back door of his own Villa 7A, and shut the door. In the unlit living room, Frankie noticed that Eugene smelled of Burma-Shave, like Champ. The irrelevant thought startled her back to her senses. She shook herself free of Eugene's grip and faced him.

"I didn't kill Gilbert Howard. Why didn't you let me stay in Villa 7B and tell the police so?"

Eugene shook his head. "Frankie, I know cops. I *am* one. Even the best policemen want a quick arrest. Many more would be happy to create a scapegoat in a high-profile case like this one. Unless the real murderer shows up and hands himself over with a bow on his nose, they've got you with *motive* and *opportunity*. All they need are *means*—a gun. With your fingerprints on it."

The only gun she'd ever had in her possession was King Samson's gun, and it remained safely somewhere out in the bushes behind Villa 7B where she'd lost it the night before. How lucky she didn't have it now. Frankie held her cold hands tight together and stared into Eugene's face, a pale moon in his darkened living room.

Such a misunderstanding as this couldn't happen. Not to the daughter of a minister, not a good neighbour who helped people where she could.

Eugene said, "The police and the papers would like nothing more than to show the world that Gilbert Howard's murderess has been brought to quick and certain justice."

"I shouldn't have run," she said. The words tasted tinny in her mouth. "I'm innocent."

"Yes, of course." Eugene peered out his front window. "But I think—and all your friends here would probably agree—that you should hide for now. If the police arrest you tonight, they won't look for the real murderer. You'll be on every front page in Los Angeles and around the world. Tried in the papers and sentenced over breakfast tables." Eugene shifted suddenly. He let go of her. "But maybe you're right, Frankie. Look, if you want to go back, I'll take you. You're a smart girl, and you may be able to talk your way out of arrest. I'll stand by you if you do, through booking and trial. I'll assure them that I believe you are innocent. All the way, Frankie."

Blankly she said, "I have to go to a screen test on Monday morning." She wrapped her arms around her own waist and held herself tight. "I'm up for the role of a sad manicurist."

She had never for a moment believed that jails would have any place in her life, but now she saw that the law could take you like a wolf in the woods when you strayed too far from home.

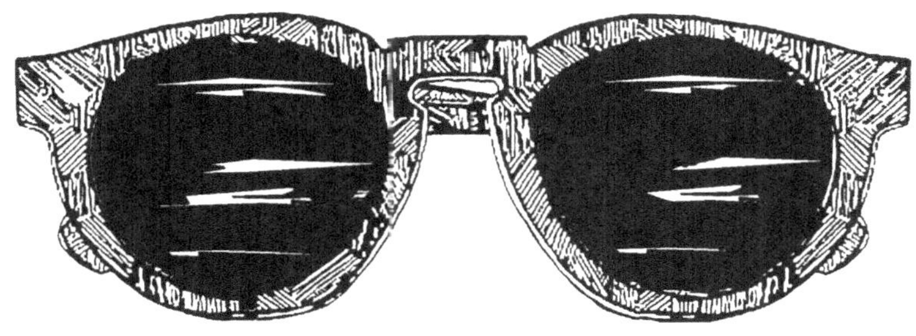

The casting call is murder

COMING SOON FROM

PULP LITERATURE PRESS

THE ABSENCE

CREATION DONE DIFFERENT

Erin Kirsh

Erin Kirsh *is a writer and performer based in Vancouver, British Columbia. Her short story* 'The Wind of a Train' *appeared in* Pulp Literature *Issue 16. A Pushcart Prize nominee, she has had her work published in* The Malahat Review, Arc Poetry Magazine, EVENT, The Dalhousie Review, CV2, QWERTY, *and* Geist. *She won* The Molotov Cocktail's *2017 Shadow Award for poetry. Visit her at erinkirsh.com or follow her on twitter @kirshwords.*

The Absence

When we look into the open casket, there is nothing
but biblical blue velvet and a golden egg sparkling

like light off a disco ball. We glance away as if it's you
in there, pale, motionless, the shrieking

pink gone from your cheeks. The mourners dressed
like monarchs. Above them, rose butterflies frozen

mid flap, suspended, and still, you too
had magnificent stillness, you too lived in between.

In the cracks of birch floor slats, dandelions wriggle
up, age into puffs then slither back through the planks

a cloud of dandelion seeds descend like tiny umbrellas
around our ankles, begin again. We hope for the same

weep in undisrupted silence, sound sucked away like spiders
into a vacuum. Instead, a ringing: melancholic

water glasses played by crone fingers, thin and sagging
lips form your name, slow tongues configure familiar letters

and when our ears begin to ache from this complicit quiet
the egg twitches, shudders. Hiccups a most minute   /crack.

Creation Done Different

Behind me they massage
the clay, knuckle it into molds
press it between blocks

until it squawks. I am misplaced
at this task, a seashell
in Saskatoon, wary about dark

magic, cakey nails. These lumps
will be corvids, they say some will break
like real baby crows

weak in the beak, flightless
and feeble and small.
How can anyone speak

so casually about nature
like, it's just the life cycle
just the food chain just

the facts. The first feathers struggle
with terracotta, hatch through
thickness, the hybrid sings

out a sickness, quiets, goes still.
The process resets. More clay.
Just nature, what we're imitating.

When it works, it works
when it doesn't, things die, a familiar
song, just creation done different.

Hands scoop soupy mud:
I am too flightless, too feeble
and too small for such truths.

DEAD OF SUMMER

R Daniel Lester

R Daniel Lester writes into the void. Sometimes the void wins. Other times the words win. He is the author of the hardboiled humour novellas Dead Clown Blues and 40 Nickels (Shotgun Honey/Down & Out Books). His short story 'Some Say the World Will End in Fire' appeared in Pulp Literature *Issue 5*. His writing, across a range of genres, has appeared in multiple publications, including Broken Pencil, 365 Tomorrows, Switchblade, Points In Case, and the clown-noir anthology Greasepaint & 45s. Previously a longtime Vancouver resident, he currently lives in Toronto with his spouse and daughter. The battle with the void continues daily.

*D*ead of Summer

The dead move beneath her window. She watches them three floors below, floating through circles of streetlamp glow like a school of tiny fish flitting just underneath the water's surface. Clearly boys, their sneakers, jeans, t-shirts. Shaved heads and curved skulls. Hungry, predatory gazes.

Her ghost stories.

They yell and moan, twitch and dance. They swing their arms in violent circles and make loud, grinding noises, which she guesses to be the frustrated gnashing of their teeth, since they are all souls of young men taken before their time.

The other residents of the building, blue-haired, blue-veined, white-dentured old women, hate the ghosts, cursing their very presence. They scream at them and pour pots of scalding hot water down onto the plaza below. Scare tactics. But their balms and creams stink with the fear of the grim reaper, so it stands to reason they want to keep the stillness from their lungs, hearts, bones — if only for a little while longer.

Really, they have more in common than they think.

The boys, dead, haunt the streets that once gave them life. The women, left behind by their men, haunt the hallways and lounges of the seniors' home, counting out their remaining days in perms, foot baths, and petty gossip.

Sunset Estates Retirement Home: six stories of concrete and age spots built smack dab in the middle of the city. Each unit, a starter casket. Learn to use less, live small, take tiny steps. Be gracious and polite, tick down like a timepiece left purposefully unwound. Perhaps not the worst way to die, but not how she once imagined it. Amelia Earhart, that's the way to go. On an adventure, eyes afire, chin up, vanish, leave a pretty memory.

Girl, never waste away slowly in plain view.

If death is the play that everyone stars in, it's the long, painful prelude she dreads, far more than the main act itself. Overstaying her welcome, shrunk down to a mad skeleton, pissing the bed and cackling nonsense. Surrounded by an army of nurses armed with uniforms and smiles so starched and crisp-white, one errant touch would shatter them into a thousand pieces.

Sunset Estates Retirement Home: six stories of concrete and aging lust. Like the dormitories of her college years, and the old folks nearly as randy. She knows the men, of which there are precious few, trade in Viagra pills like they once traded baseball cards and pin-up shots. Anyone who thinks the young have cornered the market on casual sex hasn't walked these halls on a Friday night. But she isn't interested in that anymore, not since her Harold passed.

In fact, not interested in much, except the dead boys.

She had known of many dead men — father, brother, husband, friends, a generation of soldiers, even a classmate, once upon a time. Towheaded, with a lopsided smile, he liked to pick his nose and then boldly offer the rolled-up fruits of his labour to her and the other neighbourhood girls as if a prize were to be awarded. Or maybe like a promise ring, his intentions grand and honourable. With this snot, I thee wed.

Then, one afternoon, he disappeared from the playground, not to be seen alive again. "Got took," her mother told her, never elaborating, just holding her hand tighter and taking purposeful strides as they walked from house to school, school to house, keeping a watchful eye for strangers.

Years later, she learned they'd found the boy's body three weeks after the abduction in a makeshift grave dug shallow in the industrial outskirts of the city. The ceremony was closed casket and family only.

Eighty years ago, once upon a time.

Now, her mother's long in the ground and she's in old people storage waiting for the next step in the process. That's why the ghosts don't frighten her. Instead, they are entertainment, a distraction from the routine, from days that bleed other days. And she is an excited audience of one, clapping and whistling as they whirl and spin, because everything, dead or alive, enjoys being admired. Also, she studies them, learning their ways, noting how they negotiate a world that has left them behind. Survival tactics. Because she will be joining them sooner than later.

So she listens to the boys, too, but they communicate in a strange tongue she can't comprehend. Harsh, guttural bursts that echo up to her third floor window. An ugly lullaby that lulls her into an ugly sleep, head in her arms on the windowsill.

When she wakes at dawn, she knows she has one more day upright at least. The night has not taken her and the day lacks the stones, frankly. Arms numb, neck sore, sleep pulling at her muddled thoughts like a toddler drags a stuffed animal along the floor, she looks down on the plaza — but the ghosts are not there. She is not theirs. Not yet.

And it is silent.

Proof, to her, that even the dead need sleep.

Saint Kaupas. Saint Mullen. Saint Gonzales.

Legends, so bow down.

We are skate rats. We skate to live. We live skate life.

One board, four wheels, a concrete forest. All we want. All we need.

We kick. We push. And repeat.

We fall. We get up. And repeat. Marking pavement with our skin like we spray walls with our tags. We were here. We are here.

We bleed. We sweat. We break bones. And repeat.

We hold up scraped palms and bashed elbows to the Skate Gods. See? Dues paid.

We YouTube the old skate vids and read/reread the thrashed Thrashers. Minister Phelps is our street preacher, shouting from the gaps, the banks, the 12-stairs. RIP. We listen and obey. We keep the faith. We spread the good word.

We study the masters. We learn vicarious. We imitate. We practice. We pop kickflips. We 50-50 grind. We ollie up curbs.

Saint Templeton. Saint Carroll. Saint Cardiel.

Legends, so bow down.

We film lines. We edit footage. We post clips. We get clicks. We get views.

We Snap. We Gram. We social media kings, baby.

We chat up pretty girls at the mall. We vibe good times. We vibe unavailable and skate obsessed. We vibe gone, already in love.

Summertime, so we sleep where we sleep. We crash houses. We crash couches. We sleep doubled up, tangled, but it ain't really like that. Even if it was, whatever. We don't label. We be.

We mean peace but sometimes run into war. We protect our own. We fight. We throw punches. We swing boards.

We roll in a pack. We are family.

We know the city. We are the city.

Summer is our playground.

September will never come.

We do night missions. We bomb hills — no pads, no helmets, no stress.

Shit, c'mon, we live forever.

We seek transition. We hop fences. We take necessary measures, force our environment to adapt to us. We wax curbs and Bondo cracks. We light up spots.

Sugar is fuel, so we re-up at 24-hour corner stores. We buy pop. We buy chocolate bars. We fill backpacks. We push. We shove. We throw self-serve candy. We crack jokes and act the fool. We get kicked out by pissed off clerks with no soul/zero sense of humour.

We get back to business and look for empty streets. We hunt for barren avenues. We hunger for desolate storefronts and deserted parking lots, anywhere the pavement is smooth and the overnight security guards fat/lazy/paid by the hour.

We roll in. We skate. We roll out.

We pay homage. We study sacred sites. Carlsbad. El Toro. The Davis Gap. We steeped in skate lore.

Saint Koston. Saint Dill. Saint Reynolds.

Legends, so bow down.

We know the past to know the future. We crave our own identity and carve out our own history, write our own lore.

We were here. We are here.

Future will scream our names.

We kick. We push. And repeat.

We bleed. We sweat. We break bones. And repeat.

We learn vicarious. We imitate. We practice. We improve. We pop switch tre flips. We crooked grind. We ollie gaps.

We end night missions at The Spot. Our spot, sacred to us. The plaza. Buttery ledges. A sick hubba. The 7-stair with a kinked rail that will take our balls if we're not man enough.

The Spot, next to an old folks' home, and the old ladies yell at us. They say we're noisy brats. We get flak. We overstay our welcome. They try to pour boiling water on our heads. We curse them back. We flip birds. We joke, "Grandma, why?"

They call the cops. We get hassled. If they catch us, the cops take our boards, threaten to lock us up, throw away the key. We say, "Okay, fine." We adapt. We post lookouts. We plan escape routes.

We roll in a pack. We are family.

We know the city. We are the city.

Summer is our playground.

September will never come.

The Spot, where the old ladies hate us. Except for the one. She of the open window, third floor. She never throws water. She never curses. She never calls the cops. She watches. She claps. She whistles. She knows we suffer for our art, bleed for our religion. We like her. Respect breeds respect.

We are skate rats. We skate to live. We live skate life.

Future will scream our names.

So the rule is: when cop lights paint the walls, we roll away. We run. We scatter. We wave goodnight to the old lady in the window, third floor. We bid her well.

We say, "Dream good."

JORAN'S SONG

Dave Gregory

Dave Gregory is a Canadian writer who worked on cruise ships and sailed the world for nearly two decades. He is an associate editor with the Los Angeles–based Exposition Review, and his work has appeared in numerous literary publications, including Typehouse, Firewords, and The Nashwaak Review. Follow him on Twitter @CourtlandAvenue or at courtlandavenue.wordpress.com.

Joran's Song

I knew him less than twenty-four hours. But when he died, fifteen years later, I considered him a friend.

The night we met, he had the nerve to tell me, "You're trying too hard."

My right eyebrow leapt halfway up my forehead. "Excuse me?" I was in a small but crowded hotel bar on the Greek island of Syros, ordering a second round of drinks for some women in the corner. Beside me, on a stool, sat a short dark-haired man with sun-drenched skin.

"They're backpackers. They seek adventure, not potential husbands." Clipped sentences were the best anyone could do above the blaring speakers. "You're bragging about law school. They won't remember who studied where. Or who bought drinks. They'll remember who had the cojones to dance with them."

He had a point. "Maybe. Puts me at a disadvantage, though. I can't dance."

"Madre mìa. Everyone can dance."

He dismissed my helpless shrug, told me to forget the drinks, and led me to the quieter, cooler terrace. A dozen hotel guests, talking and drinking beer, occupied tables and chairs beneath a sloped white awning. Some sat on stools at the long counter, watching reflections of city light shimmer across the bay.

"I'm Joran, from Mexico. I'll teach you moves any white boy can do."

His smile reflected innocence. I was intrigued rather than offended.

"Can you shop?" he asked.

"What?" That eyebrow again.

"Show me how you push a cart."

I played along and extended my arms, elbows slightly bent.

"Now to the beat." Joran balled his fists and reached out. His voice changed to song. "And shop. And shop." He bounced to the music coming from inside the hotel. "Top shelf on the left." He acted each line. "And put it in the cart."

I followed. Keeping one arm steady, I raised the other and reached for an imaginary overhead item, then dropped it in the pretend cart.

"Now, top shelf on the right. And put it in the cart. And shop. And shop."

Long aisles of boxed cereals, jarred sauces, and canned vegetables materialized around us.

Joran kept bouncing, every reach was a dramatic flourish until his hands returned to the tubular handle of the make-believe cart. "And shop and shop and shop," he continued singing, pushing and selecting groceries.

Three backpackers on the terrace stared and laughed. Joran's moves looked absurd until I peered through the windows and noticed the dance steps, the ones everyone inside the bar had been doing all night, weren't so different from those Joran had just taught me. His were funnier but no less graceful or rhythmic.

"Now sprinkler." Joran put the palm of his right hand behind his head and pointed the other arm in the same direction as his right elbow. "And sprinkler. And sprinkler." Pumping with his bent arm, he watched the fingers on his left hand sweep in a steady arc. Joran twisted his upper body as far as he could without shifting his feet, then stopped pumping.

"And back. Dft-dft-dft-dft-dft-dft-dft." Lips vibrating to the sound, his head bobbled. In one fluid motion, his left arm swung back to where it started.

I conjured a lush green lawn, dappled with sunlight. A thick stream of water pulsed through the air. A rainbow hovered in the mist. When I tried the move, three hotel guests accompanied me, 'sprinklering' in unison.

Next came manual lawnmowers. Joran reached low and across with one hand, then pulled back to shoulder height. Every movement seemed real and mundane, yet closely echoed the confident gyrations of those on the dance floor.

The remaining travellers on the patio moved aside tables and chairs to join us. A slight breeze drifted past. Joran's soothing voice, filled with laughter, marshalled us in time. "And start the mower. And start the mower. And shop. And shop. And shop and shop and shop. Now sprinkler. Now sprinkler. And back. Dft-dft-dft-dft-dft-dft-dft."

Our circle expanded as more joiners emerged from the bar, including the women whose drinks I'd meant to buy.

Joran declared us ready for Window Washer, Forward Thrust, and Booty Slap, which we easily perfected. If I'd known dancing could be so easy, I'd have avoided many awkward moments in darkened high school gymnasiums.

"A few more beers and you'll figure out Nipple Rub and

Helicopter Shirt on your own. ¡Ándale!" Joran led his followers inside. "This is how they'll remember you, amigo," he said to me as we stepped onto the dance floor, which we dominated for the rest of the evening.

Most guests at Hotel Chorós woke late the next morning. Tourist season was ending and many backpackers planned on catching the four o'clock ferry to Athens. Because our rooms had to be vacated by midday, nearly two dozen travellers gathered on the terrace after checkout. Many were bored, some stared across the bay, others revised or reconfirmed travel plans. Maps and guidebooks rustled; laptops and cell phones glowed.

With the bar closed until evening, no one had anything to drink except tap water from reused plastic bottles — until I burst onto the scene, carrying a case of Amstel. "I had to bribe the cleaning woman, but beer is now being served." I set the case on a wood-slatted table and ripped the cardboard open.

My friends cheered — but we lacked a bottle opener. Again, I sought the custodian but she'd disappeared and the storeroom was locked. On the terrace, several people rifled through their backpacks, conducting a futile search.

Joran arrived, his smile as bright as it was the night before. Hair slicked back, he wore white pants and a light grey button-down shirt with pink palm trees. "I may have a solution."

Removing his pack, Joran took a beer from me, then another from the case. Inverting one beverage, he wedged one cap under the pleated edge of the other and flicked his wrist. The upside-down Amstel remained intact, while a trace of mist seeped from the upright spout. Its cap bounced on the floor.

Though I'd tried the technique before, I'd never mastered it. An Australian asked, "What happens when you're down to the last one?"

"Amigo, look this way." Joran took three steps to the low stone wall separating terrace and sea. Against the edge, he hooked the cap of his remaining beer and smacked the top. With a satisfying clink, the cap fell onto the beige ceramic tile.

Joran handed both beverages to the closest adventurers, then scanned the rest of the group. "Más cerveza, por favor," he gestured with upturned hands. "Keep them coming."

The same Aussie asked, "How many ways can you open a beer?"

"I never counted."

"Let's see if you can open each one a different way."

Joran pointed at the Aussie. "I accept your challenge."

Over the next ten minutes, caps accumulated on the floor. The smiling Mexican opened one by wedging it into the door-jamb and closing the door. A fork was also used, then a knife, wedding band, coin, key, belt buckle — even the prongs from a North American computer plug. Each time, the same flick of the wrist sent a bottle top rolling across the tiles.

For the final Amstel, Joran asked if anyone had a twenty Euro note. I reached for my wallet. "As long as I get it back," I said, before handing it over.

"Of course, señor." Joran folded the bill in half, rolled it tight, then folded it again to make a v-shaped wedge. There was just enough strength in the compressed paper to pry the metal cap free.

Everyone applauded, thrilled to have cold lager on a hot day — our final day of an amazing summer on the Greek islands.

Joran sipped his beverage and returned my money. "A shame there is no more beer. Once I opened a Corona using my eye socket."

I believed him.

That afternoon, I learned Joran came from a wealthy family but had no interest in their textile business. "My goal is to never stop travelling," he said.

His next destination was Crete, the opposite direction from the rest of us. At the port, his ferry loaded and departed before ours arrived. As the boat pulled away, Joran appeared on the upper deck. Leaning against the rail, he waved across the water.

"Joran deserves a salute," I said to those waiting with me. "Drop your backpacks. It's time to dance."

Everyone followed my lead as I sang Joran's song. "Start the mower. And start the mower. And shop. And shop. And shop and shop and shop." Standing in a long line at the edge of the crowded pier, we glided through the choreography. "Now sprinkler. Now sprinkler. And back. Dft-dft-dft-dft-dft-dft-dft. Window wash, and squeegee. Nipple rub, and thrust. Take off your shirt and twirl it in the air."

While we danced the steps he taught us, Joran roared with laughter. We were in hysterics as well. Some locals looked away, some smirked, others scowled with disgust. We didn't care.

I never saw him again, but we stayed in touch. Countless pictures emerged online of Joran in various bars, never the same place twice. Over time, a growing number of videos surfaced of people performing his dance moves. When they started trickling in, I'd forward each clip to Joran and recall our evening on that sultry terrace. My friend often claimed to recognize the dancers.

Recently, Joran was among twelve Mexican tourists killed in Egypt's Western Desert. Army officials mistook a convoy of jeeps for jihadists in a restricted zone and ordered an aerial strike.

The tour company later proved the group was in a 'safe' area, where they brought guests daily to photograph the shifting sand.

Joran once said I would be remembered for my dance moves. Instead, that is *his* legacy. I hope that, before the Apache helicopters raced in, flying low over the dunes, Joran's desert convoy stopped for a break and he had time to open a beer for everyone, using as many different methods as there were people gathered round.

I hope he also had time, there in the arid, windswept landscape, to teach his group to dance. They'd be unlikely lessons in a desert, but I picture Joran, high on a sandy ridge, happy and uninhibited, leading a line of laughing travellers in the unforgettable dance moves he taught the world. "And shop. And shop. And shop and shop and shop. Now sprinkler. Now sprinkler. And back. Dft-dft-dft-dft . . . ."

PROJECTIONS

Kim Harbridge

Kim Harbridge writes strange little stories from her home in Surrey, British Columbia. Her fiction has appeared in or is forthcoming from Accenti Magazine and AE Micro, and has been awarded a Burnaby Writers' Society Prize and a Chester Macnaghten Prize. You can find her on twitter as @kimharbridge.

$\mathscr{P}$ROJECTIONS

The projector wouldn't turn on, no matter what Grant tried. He kicked the machine, more out of frustration than a sincere attempt to get the thing working. This was not what he needed tonight.

It had been a hard week. The latest predictions from the climate summit, the news of the floods in the city. He came home rattled each night, unsure how to discuss the day's new horrors with his granddaughter, or if he should even try. The girl seemed unfazed, and why shouldn't she be? She had spent her young life preparing for this world, toting emergency kits in her backpack, ducking under desks for weekly drills. She had grown up under a dark sky, was accustomed to it. She couldn't be nostalgic for something she'd never experienced.

He told himself he did it for her, the Friday night backyard ritual with the projector. But while he was out there that evening, heading into the second hour of trying to get the projector working, she was in the kitchen, eyes fixed on her phone. She hadn't even noticed this disruption of their normal routine. What little consolation the projector offered, Grant realized, it offered to him alone. He fell into the lawn chair next to the silent projector, rubbed his sore left shoulder, and looked up.

The plastic sheeting over the dome's frame fluttered loose at one seam, and between the flaps he could make out a sliver of the dark, smoggy sky overhead.

He'd seen advertisements for places you could go to see the real thing. A two-day drive up north, where there were no lights, no phones, no smokestacks, no fires. Where you could breathe clean air, sleep under a sky that resembled the one he had grown up gazing at. A sky that was impossible to see in the city.

For an exorbitant fee, of course. And for what? An overpriced campground billing itself as a sanctuary. But every time he passed the advertisements in the train station, his eyes lingered.

Maybe if they ate less bio-meat, put off phone upgrades until next year …

He could already see his granddaughter's nose wrinkle at the suggestion. No new phone *again*? She'd never go for it.

On the table beside the projector, his phone lit up with an incoming message. He could see it was from his granddaughter. Texting from the kitchen, rather than opening the window to holler out at him. With a shake of his head, he reached for his phone, his hand brushing the projector's power cord. The cable jostled loose from its socket, fell down onto the artificial turf.

Grant frowned down at the machine. Bypassing his phone, he reached for the power cord. He studied it for a moment, looked at the projector, then fitted the end of the cable snugly into the side of the machine.

He swiped away the message from his granddaughter without reading it. If he had, he would have seen, in a mix of letters and emojis, that she was asking why there were no stars tonight.

Grant's breath picked up with anticipation as he pressed the button on his phone that activated the projector's programming.

The machine rattled to life, the lens cover retracted, and the inside of the dome bloomed bright with artificial starlight.

The kitchen window scraped open, and his granddaughter, her gaze cast upwards, leaned out to get a better view. Grant watched her as she watched the sky.

Maybe next year, the sanctuary. For now, they had this steady spray of artificial starlight between them and the low-hanging sky, a small defence against a vast and empty dark of their own making.

It would have to be enough.

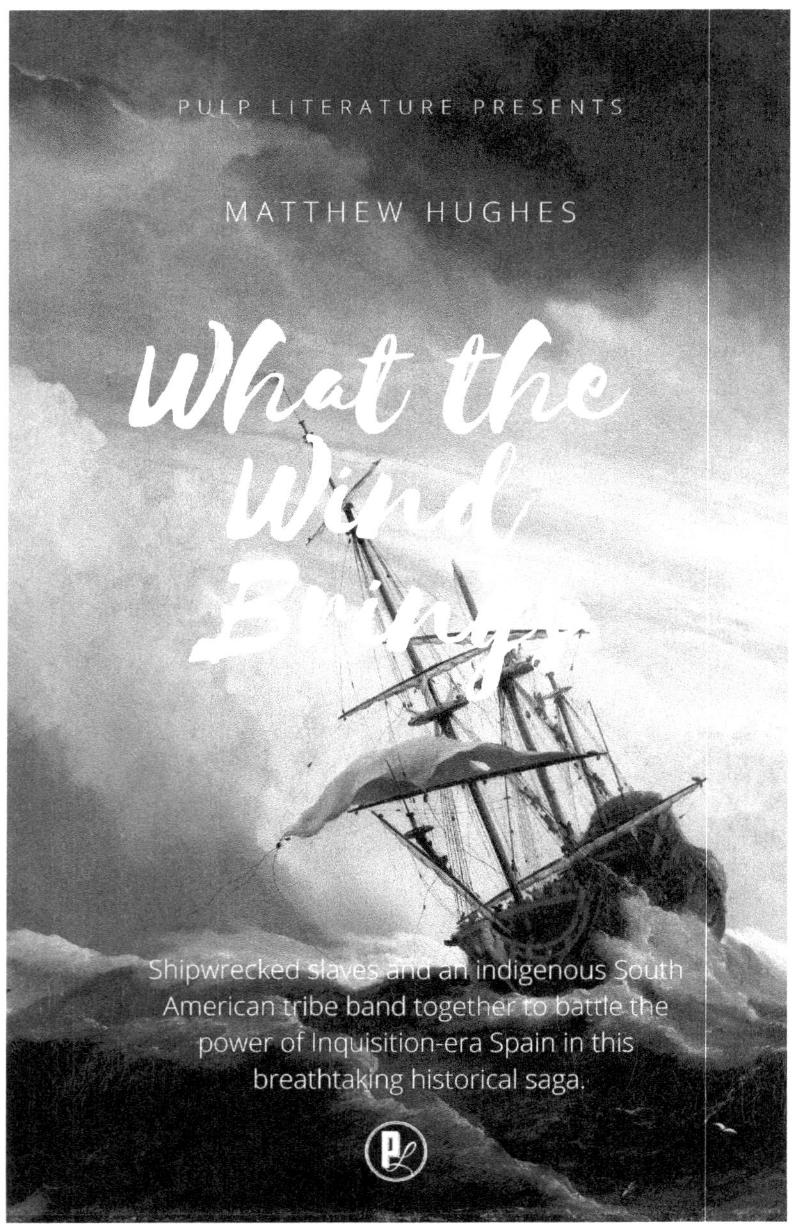

ORDER YOUR LIMITED-EDITION SIGNED HARDCOVER NOW
pulpliterature.com/the-bookstore/what-the-wind-brings

LIKE WE SAID

Peter Norman

Peter Norman's work has appeared in The Walrus, Best Canadian Poetry, and elsewhere. His short story 'The Night Stylist' was published in Pulp Literature Issue 12, Autumn 2016. He is the author of a novel, Emberton, and four poetry collections. Learn more at peternorman.ca.

Like We Said

When you wake up, dried crud on your tongue,
and rise and fumble through the door,
your temple striped where it was pressed too long
against a corduroy davenport,
having told us you intended to lie down
a quarter hour or less, and now we're gone
and every room is empty in the house
and every street abandoned and the long
crazed shriek of a derailing train
is all the noise in the entire night —
don't fret. It's what we meant when we kept saying
everything was going to be all right.

THE LION

Hannah van Didden

Hannah van Didden writes where the story takes her — usually somewhere dark but truthful and often beautiful. You will find pieces of her in places such as Tahoma Literary Review, Crannóg, Southerly Literary Journal, Breach, Atticus Review, Southword Journal, and thirtyseven.

The Lion

A lion walked into a management consultancy. He said to the guy at the front desk, "I want to see the man in charge."

The man in charge turned out to be a woman.

"What is it you want?" said the woman in charge.

"Just a little of your time," said the lion, shaking out his mane. The woman had a thick middle and shapely loins, like his last gazelle. He would have to work hard to keep his focus.

"Time is money, you know, and my charge-out rate is extreme."

"I spent all my money on the plane trip from Africa and the in-flight magazine told me your firm was the best."

She eyed him over tortoiseshell rims. "I'll give you five minutes."

"I thank you for that, The lion dipped his head, "because I want to learn how to be a success."

"What do you mean by success?" she said.

"I want to be successful in this … machine." The lion flourished a front paw up and out; the woman's gaze followed its movement from the glass-coated sky to the dark and art-heavy walls.

"We're in a foyer." She scrunched her eyebrows at him.

"Successful in business," the lion said, slowly and deliberately.

"You're a lion." She reflected his tone, talked down her nose. "Why would you want, or need, to be successful in business?"

"I've been doing some reading," the lion replied. "It seems to me that until I set myself up in a developed country, exist in accordance with its systems, and attach some fiscal KPIs, my life won't have value."

"I cannot disagree." She looked at him intently. "Do you have any services to offer? Anything you could sell?"

"Not really." The lion stroked his chin. "I see no real benefit to being ogled in a cage, à la my zoo-bound countrymen. And my particular skills are jungular, associated mainly with open-space stalking and killing. For food, of course." He chuckled to himself and patted his rumbling belly. "Only hunt for food."

"Speaking of hunting, there is always the value of your pelt." The woman did not bat an eyelid when she suggested it. "But I suppose you want to live."

"That would be helpful, yes."

"A shame," said the woman. "And I would help you further, however, your time is up."

"You're harsh! My watch says it's been only four minutes —"

"The business world is harsher than the jungle."

"— and you've been rather vague as to what I can do," said the lion who, in spite of his words, was starting to get an inkling of what it was that would bring him business success.

"All right," said the woman. "I like to think I'm fair. I'll think on that a bit longer for you."

"I'll give you five minutes," said the lion, unsheathing his claws — but in four, he was on the terrace with a pop-up stall, selling chunks of free-range meat and salted crackling.

CULINARY SUBJUGATION

Jakob Drud

Jakob Drud lives in Aarhus, Denmark, with his two children. He's been writing for the last twenty years and has a passion for fiction that surprises, brings new insights, and makes him laugh. The fantastic genres are all that and more, so many of his stories are science fiction, fantasy, or something in between. Links to his stories can be found at jakobdrud.com, and you can find him on twitter as @jakobdrud, if tweets about writing and life are your thing.

Culinary Subjugation

Joseph Campton sent his resignation to the Preserve council while sitting in the corner booth farthest from the counter in Hu Wong's diner. Then he packed away his Grid console and stirred the coffee, mixing low-fat milk and artificial sweetener into the brown liquid. The taste had a calming effect on his nerves, and he realized that Hu Wong had once again gotten his hands on real coffee beans. How he got them through the irradiated lands, or what place on Earth was still clean enough to grow quality Java, Campton couldn't begin to guess.

Hu came over to the table, smiled, and asked, "Everything all right this morning, Mr Campton?"

"The coffee's great, Hu."

"Thank you, Mr Campton. It's a pleasure to have you here." Hu bowed and left for another table.

Good as the coffee was, Hu Wong was the real reason Campton came here. Hu always conveniently forgot Campton's title of food inspector, and sometimes his perfect manners even allowed Campton to forget the job himself.

Today the illusion burst despite Hu's grace. Halfway through the coffee, Campton's Grid console beeped. With rising anger, he read the council's answer.

"We regret to inform you that we cannot accept your resignation. The workforce in the Preserve is short-handed, and therefore we all have to bear our part of the burden. Furthermore, we forbid you to resign again. The Pitonians asked specifically for your services, and it is the opinion of the council that you affront them by not accepting the honour they bestow on you."

He threw the Grid console into his briefcase and got up. Hu came over, shook his hand, and collected the tip Campton had left for him.

"Would you believe that?" Campton said. "The Pitonians value my services."

"I'm sorry to hear that, Mr Campton."

"Thank you, Hu. You're too kind."

Campton left Hu's and walked outside under the domed sky. Across the street, a guy was pissing on the handle of his car. Nothing marked the vehicle as belonging to a food inspector, but people in the Preserve knew it on sight by now. Clutching the handle of his briefcase a little harder, Campton crossed the street.

"Take that, Pit-lover," the man shouted. The words came out slurred with drink. Campton recognized him as one of the Horowitzes, a family that made it out of Boston before the Pitonians nuked the city. They had a moonshine still in the backyard that he'd checked about a month ago.

"You shouldn't be drinking your own booze," Campton said. "I found wood spirit in it."

"Pits drink it, inspector-man," Horowitz said. He zipped up and took a few wobbly steps into the middle of the street.

"The Pitonians drink anything. Doesn't mean you can." Campton rummaged through his pockets and found a greasy paper napkin that he used to wipe the handle. Keeping an eye on Horowitz, he unlocked the door and got in behind the wheel.

"I know your car. Someday I'll blow it up."

You can't, Campton thought, *the Pitonians took our explosives.* Probably ate them, too. The thought didn't make him feel any safer, though. With all that ethanol in his backyard still, Horowitz could easily cook up a nice firebomb.

Campton rolled down the window. "Look, Horowitz, I'm just a man with a job. A man."

"I read *Soylent Green*, inspector. And so did you."

Horowitz's middle finger waved Campton on his merry way.

The stink of piss through the open window mixed with fresh air as Campton left the town and drove into the countryside. The engine ran erratically, black smoke puffing from the exhaust. It had been a long time since the council had been allowed to send scavengers into the radiated lands, and the spare machinery parts they had brought back were used up by now.

Nobody dared to leave the Preserve anymore. The Pitonian pre-invasion nukes had poisoned the atmosphere, and rumour had it that armed Pitonians had occupied the whole solar system, turning it into a giant war-factory. Far more colourful rumours abounded, but Campton had chosen his version of reality a long time ago. It remained as unconfirmed as did everything else about the Pitonians.

He eyed the dome through the windshield. It stretched across the Preserve, shielding the humans inside from the radioactive ashes of the invasion, and today it sported a bright sun and a moderate build-up of clouds on the eastern horizon. That might change during the day, but for now the Pitonian technicians seemed satisfied to let the Preserve population enjoy a false Indian summer.

With one elbow on the wheel, Campton checked his orders. Five farms before lunch, five after. *Crops and dairy*, he thought, but then remembered that one farm had a small lake on the premises. He'd have to check for frogs and mosquito larvae in case the Pitonians wanted a new specialty. Inspecting farms would be about as pleasant as talking with Horowitz. He gripped the wheel.

Around noon, Campton pulled up at Juan Alvarez' farm, the fifth on his list. The only greeting he got was from the snarling family dog, pregnant and heavy but healthy-looking. He noted the dog's status in the inspection report on his Grid console.

"Mr Alvarez," he called out of the car window. "Please put a leash on your dog."

Juan Alvarez appeared in the doorway of his barn, wiping manure from his hands onto his threadbare overalls. Didn't wipe them all that effectively either, Campton noted, before Juan extended his hand.

"Cows again? Or are you here for the wife?"

Campton merely took his console and opened the door. "The dog," he reminded Juan.

"Just because my farm is food country for your alien friends doesn't mean you can tell me what to do with my animals." He got a grip on the dog's collar. "Barn or bed?"

"Isn't she up and around yet?" Campton tried to keep his voice neutral, but Juan's grimace made sympathy well up in him, despite everything.

"Very hard birth. She'll be in bed for at least another week." Juan pressed a dirty hand down on Campton's shoulder. "Just you remember what she went through."

"Barn, then," Campton said, and Juan removed his hand.

The inspection went smoothly, even if Juan kept complaining.

"Why do you come around again? It's only two months since your last visit, and it's not as if the Pitonians care what they eat."

Campton used a dipper from the console to test a cowpat. According to the readings it qualified for the Pitonian cuisine, but the why of it beat him. Their feeding habits were as shrouded in mystery as the contents of their thrice-damned cookbooks.

"I don't think they eat just everything. It could be that the manure is for Pitonians of lower social status, and the beef is for the officers."

"Hope it's the other way round," Juan grumbled.

Campton continued to note that the cows had been well fed. The number of stillborn and mutated calves figured lower than average for the Preserve, but that might be because the Pitonians had lowered the radiation levels in the dome lately. "Your barn passes the test, Juan."

"Of course it does. I work my ass off here to supply those yellow-skinned blimps with beef, and I get nothing but a sore back since my John Deere broke down."

"I'm just the inspector. Take it up with the council."

"I'm taking it up with you. You come around here bitching with me all the time, but there's never any help. I asked for parts for the tractor months ago."

"Juan."

"You're just doing the council's dirty work, making sure everybody behaves!"

"I try to help," Campton said defensively. "Keep an eye out for hints, you know. Liza figured maybe we could find out what quality food means to the Pitonians … We need to keep the kids safe."

"And look where that got Liza." Juan glared at him triumphantly.

Campton clenched his fist so hard around the Grid console that it creaked, and in a red-hazed instant he imagined breaking the plastic casing over Juan's head. "I'm through with the cattle. I'd like to see your wife now."

"You son of a bitch," Juan shouted. He ran his hands through his hair. "Look, I'm sorry I mentioned Liza. Sorry, OK?"

Campton stared at him.

"Please, can't you just say you saw her and the baby, and something was wrong. I don't know, some kind of mutation on the kid or something? I'll pay you whatever you want, just fake the report. Who would know anyway?"

"I have to check."

Without warning, Juan punched Campton in the nose. The blow sent him sprawling, and a blurred second later he looked up at Juan from a pile of manure.

"That nose won't cause you half the pain my wife suffered. Remember that when you file your report, you prick."

Campton got up and wiped the blood from his face with his sleeve. He would not forget.

The car's suspension protested his haste as he left Juan's farm along the bumpy dirt road. Well out of sight of the Alvarez farm, he stopped and was violently sick on the edge of the road, just short of the first row of cornstalks.

"Why the hell did he talk that way about Liza?" Campton mumbled. He spat bile and stomach acid on the ground. "It's his own goddamn fault I wrote that report."

Everybody knew Campton and Liza had been lovers, and people like Juan used that to hurt him every chance they got. Thinking about Liza's death made him sick again, and the heaving called water to his eyes. Just tears from the strain, not tears of sorrow, he told himself. He had cried enough of the latter when the council forced him to succeed her as food inspector.

"I can't do this anymore," he whispered to the cornstalks.

A bleep from his Grid console drew him back to the car. It was a council demand for two extraordinary inspections. One was for Piton Prime, the Pitonian restaurant, and the inspection, needlessly flagged 'urgent', was a special demand by the alien chef himself. Campton felt nausea return.

The other inspection was at Hu's, flagged 'today', just a step below urgent. Campton's heart started to throb, until he recalled how the council loved to make people run needlessly pressing errands to prove their power. At least they had made it easy to do their bidding this time. He'd planned on having lunch at Hu's anyway. He needed to see a friendly face for a change.

Several restaurateurs had complained that official examinations scared away the guests, so as per his usual on-duty routine Campton took the kitchen entrance. Hu's wife gave his dirty clothes only a fleeting glance when he stepped inside.

"Inspection?" she asked.

"I'm sorry about the inconvenience." He covered his swollen nose. The Wongs would be nervous enough about the surprise inspection. No need to call attention to the violent part of his job.

"Wait a minute," Mrs. Wong instructed him and disappeared into the back room. A moment later she returned and gently pressed an ice-filled towel to his swollen nose. "They shouldn't hit you."

"Thanks." Campton thought how special she was, and not for the first time he wondered if there were any people alive outside the Preserve. There had to be. If the Wongs could serve him genuine coffee, there must be an outside source.

"Want me to show you around, Mr Campton?" she asked.

"If it's not too much trouble."

"Never for you, Mr Campton."

She let him take samples from the freezers and fridges before showing him their dry goods and the live-animal cages and fish tanks. He compared the living conditions of the carp and shrimp to the optimal standards set by the Pitonians, noting that both the pH level of the water and the number of live plants in the tank were perfect. The number of carp was in accordance with Pitonian prescription, the fish appeared to be fed regularly, and the residue of fish fodder in the water was within the acceptable range. Only one tank had a problem: it contained an excess of three giant shrimp.

"For your lunch," Mrs Wong said. "Deep fried with the house sour-sweet." He started to hold up his hand at the mention of deep fry, but she insisted. "A belly won't do you any harm, Mr Campton."

That's what people said to Liza, he thought, but Mrs Wong already had a net out. Three of the Wong kids swarmed into the kitchen while she was fishing, and for the first time since he entered, Mrs Wong stopped smiling. Campton winked at her.

"Hey, kids. How are you?" Campton asked. "All of you still got three arms?"

The youngest, a boy of four, grinned as if Campton were joking. "No," he shouted. "Just two."

His oldest sister corrected him. "Remember what Mommy said. When Mr Campton's here, we all have three arms." She waved at Campton with her two hands, then retracted the right into her T-shirt and waved at him through the neck. The boy laughed and struggled to follow her example.

"Sorry to see your kids are mutants, Mrs Wong," Campton said. "I'll note that in my report."

"Thank you, Mr Campton. You're too kind."

Campton inspected another three farms before finding the courage to take the twenty-mile drive to Piton Prime, at the edge of the dome. A lichen-grey storm was brewing in the northern sky, but he had no way to tell if it would end up as a breeze or a gale. The Pitonian technicians guided the weather much like nature had done before the invasion: with randomness and impunity.

Piton Prime. The restaurant at the end of the world. Campton parked the car on a flat dirt expanse only ten metres from the dome wall. The three-story architecture looked impossible, roof and walls supported by twisted pillars that narrowed to toothpick thinness at the base. He'd seen the silent, hovering shocktanks that protected the council's headquarters, so he knew the Pitonians could suspend gravity. But whenever he saw the restaurant, he thought it would fall over and crush him.

He sat for a while in the car, legs shaking, hands clammy on the wheel. Seven months ago he had parked in this exact spot. Liza had been shaking just like he did now.

"I can learn about their selection process," she had said. "I know I can, and when I do, we'll know how to cheat them."

He had begged her not to go in, but she didn't listen. If she were here now, she would enter the restaurant all over again just to give people in the Preserve a better chance of survival.

On oatmeal legs, Campton got out of the car.

The entrance was a twisted, quadrilateral hole in the wall, covered only by a shimmering field of light. Campton couldn't see past the curtain of light, and when he stepped through, the portal immediately took him to a strange kitchen. Globules of fire hovered in the air, with spits and metal containers hanging alongside, boiling and sizzling. Twenty to thirty Pitonians floated in mid-air, cleaning and chopping, knives and instruments shifting between loose-jointed limbs that could bend in several directions. Campton had never seen so many Pitonians in one place.

A huge, spherical Pitonian with nine arms floated over to Campton. Its skin was pale yellow, and like the rest of the Pitonians its circular body had two large orifices, one of which contained rows and rows of spiky teeth.

"Ah. The inspector," it said. "I'm the chef." The unexpected English sounded from an unseen speaker. A translator. The human voice was friendly and cheerful in a British kind of way, but Campton detected a Midwestern accent.

"I hope I don't come at an inopportune moment," Campton said. With sweaty palms, he took the console from his pocket and started a new report. "What do you want me to inspect?"

"Everything. We have important visitors tonight."

"Let's start with your live animals, then," Campton suggested, ready to change his mind if the chef showed the least displeasure.

Light flickered around them, and a dizzying moment later, Campton found himself in an acrid-smelling room filled with cages of live creatures. Some of the animals had scales, some fur; a few had plumes of feathers or leathery carapaces. But other than these traits, they bore no resemblance to earthly life. Strange limbs protruded at impossible angles, and Campton wondered briefly what kind of evolutionary pressures had brought forth such monstrosities. The same harsh conditions that had shaped the Pitonians, he supposed.

On his console, Campton brought up a long list of information on the animals' optimal living conditions, then checked the cages one by one, carefully avoiding the animals labelled 'deadly' or 'poisonous'. Working silently, he thought about the questions he should ask. The tailored weather. The strange job functions that the Pitonians insisted on. The supply of food that was so much more varied than the agricultural products in the Preserve would allow for. Somewhere in all this was the key to understanding the Pitonians that Liza had searched for.

"I'm done with the animals. I'd like to see your Terran produce now."

"Ah, but of course," the chef said through its translator. The room shimmered again, turning into a smaller storage space. Sacks of flour were stacked against one wall, crates of fruit against others, and caged animals and fish tanks took up most of the floor. Sacks of whole-bean Arabica hovered in the air above large cans of powdered cocoa.

"The coffee," Campton said. "Point of origin?"

"Why, our excellent orbital factories."

"This was not —" He cleared his throat, and the words finally came out, a prayer not a question. "I thought you produced them in another Preserve."

"Oh, for heaven's sake, no! Too many humans would only disturb our war efforts. We deemed one Preserve sufficient."

Campton felt the wholesome, roasted smell of the coffee beans tickle his nose even as his soul caved in under the chef's news, and for a moment he had to reach out to support himself. Somehow he managed to pull himself together and start weighing the coffee beans.

"Why bother producing this?" Campton asked.

"We set up the Preserve to allow a token continuation of Terran life," the chef said. "Anything else would have been uncivilized. Coffee seemed a natural part of human life, fulfilling your physiological and psychological needs. Allowing animals to live in their natural elements brings out the taste. We took inspections a step further to ensure quality."

"But how does control improve the quality?" Campton asked. "It only makes people insecure." The question was dangerous, he sensed, but he had to ask. Quality seemed to be a key word to the chef.

"Well, didn't you know, old chap? Our scouts reported a human obsession with control. Your societies were filled with identity papers, laws, regulations, and surveillance. We deduced that humans have a psychological need to control everything around them. Except perhaps the weather."

Your scouts were wrong, Campton thought. *Oh man, they were wrong.* But he didn't shake his head, and he didn't say these thoughts out loud. "Let's go back to the kitchen," he suggested.

The room shimmered, and the din of the kitchen returned, along with the Pitonian cooks. Campton collected samples of different foodstuffs, but mainly he just looked around. This time he noted the differences among the Pitonians in the kitchen.

Those who cleaned vegetables only had five arms, whereas a six-armed Pitonian, cutting a hovering chunk of meat into pieces, sent the five-arms scurrying to find him new instruments.

Arms, Campton thought. *They rank themselves by arms.*

The more, the better, it seemed. He could fake a lot of reports with this knowledge and really help the kids. Especially if he could get the obviously powerful chef to help him.

He took a closer look at the meat that the six-armed cook was working. It looked like a calf, but its small head was out of proportion to the huge body.

"You eat stillborn calves?" Campton asked. "Mutants?" He thought of the caged Pitonian animals and their surplus limbs. *Could they be mutants*, he wondered, *shipped through space at god knew what cost?*

"Mutants are a rare delicacy, reserved only for the finest guests," the chef said. "The military commanders supervising the war efforts will be dining here tonight. Thankfully, your inspections have provided us with some very beneficial mutations lately."

"I haven't," Campton said. "Radiation causes genetic mutations, stillbirth, and sometimes mutated limbs. But that has nothing to do with my inspections."

"But after you took over from your predecessor, the human race showed new signs of evolution. We believe your role as inspector is the only altered variable. Now, under your care, mutations occur spontaneously in children already born. In particular, the Chinese-American variety shows signs of gastronomical virtue. Their third arm is a pleasant surprise."

A dizzy spell made Campton stagger, and he bumped into a plate left on a tabletop. It fell to the floor, and a five-armed cook turned on Campton, arms stretched out as if to strangle him.

Only a lionlike growl from the chef, untranslated, made the cook back off.

"I'm so sorry, but they aren't … " He stopped when the chef's tongue licked its toothy mouth.

"Food inspector." The chef's translator drew out the first word. "If not for your work, such mutations would never have occurred, and I would have been hard-pressed to compose a truly civilized dinner for my commanders. As long as you continue to deliver such results obediently, I won't replace you like I did your predecessor. She asked so many questions."

It should have given Campton some sort of peace to know that Liza had died trying to understand the Pitonians, but the chef's words only made him furious. Liza had devoted her life to saving the children in the Preserve, and the chef had killed her for it. She probably screamed at him until the last moment too, and Campton envied her courage. He'd been the Preserve council's willing collaborator, resigning every now and then, but always returning to do their dirty work. Even now he was too cowardly to sacrifice himself for a few kids who would end their days in the restaurant sooner or later.

He told himself that it didn't matter if the Wongs stayed happy a while longer. He told himself that his death would achieve no more than Liza's.

Still, he knew he had to try something, or he would spend the rest of his days hating himself into an early grave.

"You think that's a mutation?" he said. "That a few kids with extra arms are a sign of evolution? You can serve them to your bosses if you like, but I doubt they'll find them to their taste."

"So would I please be kind enough to serve something else?" the chef said, the translator sounding spiffy and cheerful. "My dear inspector, your predecessor invented many strange excuses to save human offspring."

"But it's just three kids. Why not try something radically different? Surely improvisation is within your … your … your unsurpassed culinary range?"

With a jolt of hope, Campton noted a short hesitation before the chef answered. "Your point?"

Campton forced himself to breathe. "Chef, I've seen the animals in your storage. They didn't go through evolution sitting inside a glass ball. Open the dome. Let humans spread out, see what we can do with the irradiated lands, and see what it can do with us."

The Preserve, with its steady food supply, would be hard to leave. The Pitonians would hunt them, and the nuclear fallout would slowly burn their lungs and bone marrow. But at the very least the kids wouldn't go to the restaurant at the end of the world.

"Your council would disagree," the chef said, as if reading Campton's mind.

"You and I know the council isn't concerned about quality. They only care about control."

The Pitonian chef regarded him for another while, and with the briefest of bobs of its floating body set the world spinning. Campton found himself standing by the restaurant's exit, facing his car.

The dome of the Preserve was gone. Where the sky had touched the ground, Campton saw pillars and arches and open space that made him think of exits from a gladiatorial arena.

He picked up his communicator and called Hu Wong. "Grab your kids," he said. "Pack up, hoof it, escape the Preserve. We're free."

From the other end, he heard only breathing. It lasted long enough to make Campton wonder if he would spend the rest of his life friendless, antagonized for destroying humanity's last sanctuary. Only when he opened the door to the car did he hear Hu clear his throat over the communicator and say, "Thank you, Mr Campton. You're too kind."

CAPTAIN HERO WAS A FEMINIST

NRM Roshak

NRM Roshak *writes all manner of things, including (but not limited to) short fiction, kidlit, and non-fiction. Her short fiction has appeared in* Flash Fiction Online, On Spec, Daily Science Fiction, Future Science Fiction Digest, *and elsewhere, and was awarded a quarterly Writers of the Future prize. She studied philosophy and mathematics at Harvard and has written code, blogged, and wrangled databases for dot-coms, Harvard, and a Fortune 500 company. She shares her Canadian home with a small family and a revolving menagerie of Things In Jars. You can find more of her work at nrmroshak.com and follow her on Twitter at @nroshak.*

Captain Hero Was a Feminist

Welcome to your first assignment for English 100X: English for Supers! You're going to write a persuasive essay on the super-hero of your choice, using the Five-Paragraph Essay Format. This guide will show you what to write in each paragraph of your essay, using examples that argue for the feminism of the Tri-State area's leading super from 2021–2025, Captain Hero.

The first paragraph is your thesis statement. For example: *Captain Hero was a champion of women's rights as well as a crime-fighter.* Keep it simple, but if you're feeling ambitious, you can jazz it up a bit. *Captain Hero wasn't just a hero in the fight against crime; he was also a hero in the fight against gender discrimination.* Don't go so far as to make it rhyme.

Put some arguments that prove your thesis in the second paragraph, like this: *Captain Hero was the first male hero in the Tri-State Super League to choose a female Chief Sidekick. He also led the League in equitable hiring practices, as over 70% of his new intern and sidekick hires were female.* Try to present three strong arguments. This isn't the place to get bogged down with quibbles, like the number of those interns and sidekicks that are rumoured to have quit in tears. You'll clear those up later in the essay.

The third paragraph is your chance to stack up the evidence *against* your thesis. Don't forget to make a transition into your first piece of counter-evidence. E.g. *However, Captain Hero's feminist reputation may seem to be belied by the seven sexual harassment suits filed against him.* You can stitch your sentences together with conjunctive adverbs: *Furthermore, female supervillains Miss Anthropy and Angela Death publicly called him out for 'inappropriately sexual' behaviour during hand-to-hand combat.* This paragraph should make your thesis look bad. But don't worry; the next paragraph will make up for it.

Devote the fourth paragraph to destroying every claim you made in the third paragraph. Transition words will come in handy here again: *Still, not a single rumour of misconduct has been substantiated. Likewise, every harassment suit against Captain Hero has settled out of court with sealed records, making it impossible to judge the merit of their claims. In contrast, Captain Hero's positive employment practices are a matter of public knowledge.* Make your fourth-paragraph case as strongly as you can. When you can't refute a counterpoint, sow doubt and confusion: *Miss Anthropy and Angela Death's reluctance to press charges has cast suspicion on their public claims.* Again, this isn't a place to bring up quibbles, such as supervillains' natural reluctance to set foot in a police station. It is, however, a good place for attacks on the source(s) of any difficult-to-refute third-paragraph statements: *Further, Miss Anthropy and Angela Death, being supervillains, are known liars and troublemakers, with every reason to defame the character of a hero they couldn't bring down in combat.*

By the time you come to the fifth paragraph, your thesis statement should be looking good again. All you need to do here is restate it, summarize the positive arguments from the second paragraph, and remind the reader that you've squelched all the doubts that the third paragraph raised. *Captain Hero's support for gender equity was demonstrated both by his hiring practices and by the genuine advancement opportunities for female supers that existed in his organization. The unsubstantiated claims made by jealous villains in an attempt to smear his character are far outweighed by his public record. Truly, Captain Hero was not just a hero, but a feminist.* Don't forget to use transition words.

Congratulations! You now know how to write a five-paragraph persuasive essay. You should, of course, choose your own superhero and your own thesis for your essay. If possible, use an example from your own budding career as a super. Squelching accusations from jealous nobodies may seem like a distraction, but it's necessary if you want to stay in the fight against crime. Otherwise, you may find yourself unfairly sidelined into another career.

I look forward to reading your essays.

~ Professor (Cpt.) Hero

HE WHO CAN OPEN ALL DOORS

Crystal Bourque

Crystal Bourque is a dark fantasy author based out of Toronto, Canada. She is obsessed with all things fantastical, so much so that she has a recurring dream about being a princess with a sword. When she's not busy writing, she loves trying new recipes, plotting her next travel destination, and singing loudly. 'He Who Can Open All Doors' won an honourable mention for the 2019 Surrey International Writers' Conference Storyteller Award.

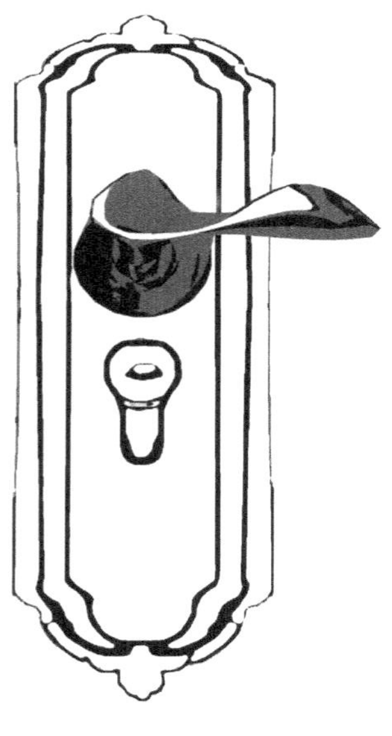

*H*E WHO CAN OPEN ALL DOORS

Sergeant Paul Frost stumbled out of the house, onto the porch, and into the sunlight. He heard his partner's boots scuff along the wood behind him. "Well, I ain't never seen nothing like that."

Dale Hunter stood on the porch, worrying his bottom lip between his teeth. The grizzled veteran had seen some pretty nasty shit over the course of his thirty-year career. Paul had heard the stories, admired the man, and considered it an honour to learn from the best.

If what they had seen inside the house had crawled under Hunter's tough hide, Paul figured it was a blessed, goddamn miracle he still managed to stand on his own two feet.

The putrid stench of rotting flesh had followed him outside, accompanied by the memory of the decomposing corpse they had found on the floor in the living room. The chest cavity had been ripped open like a birthday present.

Neither he nor Hunter had found the telltale signs of a break-in or struggle. The only evidence, apart from the body, came from a rust-coloured smear coating the doorknob of a nearby closet.

The crime scene reeked of déjà vu — the horrible, pungent kind that made Paul want to scratch his nose clean off.

"You alright?" Hunter asked.

"Yeah, sorry," he managed to say. "I've just never seen anything like … *that* before."

"You and me both," Hunter said. Paul watched him lift his hat to wipe the sweat from his brow. "Want me to handle the interview with the Crone?" He jammed the hat back onto his head and gestured with his chin to the neighbouring house.

Paul turned in time to see the curtain twitch closed. "No," he said before he sighed and scuffed the toe of his boot against dry earth. "I really wish you wouldn't call her that."

"When you explain why she's our key witness every damn time something fucked up happens in my town, I'll call her otherwise," Hunter told him. He pursed his lips and looked as though he wanted to add something, but thought better of it.

Paul shifted his weight from one foot to the other and squinted at the neighbouring home.

He supposed the general population might wonder how anyone still lived inside. With its broken shutters, cracked siding, and layers of peeling paint, it looked completely abandoned.

Which is exactly what Aunt Agnes intended, he reasoned. "Let me talk to her first," he said aloud. He watched the hesitation flicker across Hunter's face. "Please," he added.

Hunter glanced back at the house, where they had left the CSI unit to their work. "Fine, but do it now, before someone notices you've gone," he said, his voice quiet. He left Paul with a shake of his head.

Paul's nerves thrummed as he approached his aunt's house. The porch steps groaned under his weight, but he made it to the top without falling through. The door seemed much too big for such a small structure. Fixed to the wood by a thin nail was a little doll. Made of straw, it wore an orange tunic. A short length of thin red string had been tied around its waist. The doll's long arms stretched out in either welcome or warning.

He never could decide which.

A dark shadow streaked across his peripheral vision. Hand on his gun, he half crouched, half turned on still unsteady legs.

He saw nothing but sunburnt grass and cracked earth, and yet despite this, he knew he wasn't alone.

Paul took a breath and rang the doorbell.

A moment later, he heard the lock slide back before the door swung open. He found himself looking down at a woman with a cap of white hair coiled tightly into a thin bun on the top of her head.

He dug deep to find the patience he needed to tread lightly.

"Aunt Agnes," he said, taking off his hat. "I'm sorry to bother you."

"It's been ten months and five days since I last saw you." She blinked up at him through cat-eye frames. "I'm surprised you remember my name."

"Do you have a minute?" he asked, and tried not to think about what he'd seen today.

Aunt Agnes poked her head out the door. She took one look at the cruiser before taking his hand. "Why don't you come on in," she said, and pulled him across the threshold. "You look as though you could use a cold drink, and I've got just the thing." She left him to shut the door and shuffled toward the fridge.

One glance at her spotless floors had him wiping his boots on the tiny doormat. "Please don't," he told her before he entered the kitchen, hat clutched between both hands. His gaze swept over the clean but yellowed backsplash tiles, empty sink basin, and wood-burning stove. "This shouldn't take long."

"I haven't seen you since the Taylor twins went missing last year." She emerged from the fridge with a glass pitcher in one hand. "You'll sit and have some tea." Ice rattled in dark liquid as she set the pitcher on the counter.

"Well, I—"

"Go and wash up," she interrupted.

"Hold on, now—"

"And be quick about it." She somehow managed to relieve him of his hat and nudge him across the floor at the same time. When he reached the doorway on the other side of the kitchen, she gestured with a liver-spotted hand. "Bathroom's at the end of the hall."

"I *know*," he mumbled, but he did as she asked. *She's a key witness in a murder investigation,* he reminded himself as he strode to the bathroom. *Just because she's family doesn't mean . . .* He frowned when he reached the sink and turned around.

The bathroom didn't have a door.

He hesitated before stepping back to take a closer look at the rooms he'd passed. He frowned at Aunt Agnes's bedroom and then at what had been his room as a child.

All of the doors had been removed. Even from the closets.

Clean hands forgotten, he stormed back into the kitchen. "Don't tell me *you* released him!" he said.

"Sweet merciful Goddess." She set the biscuit tin on the counter so hard it made him wince. She turned to face him with a look that pinned him where he stood. "How could you possibly think I would *do* such a thing?" The tops of her cheeks turned a bright shade of pink.

"Because *someone* set him free," he told her in a strained voice. "I've got a dead body just next door and a partner who thinks you've got something to do with it." He bent down so that they were eye to eye and let his unasked question hover in the air between them.

Aunt Agnes pushed her glasses up onto the bridge of her nose. Her nostrils flared. "Come with me," she said, prodding him aside to head for the front door.

Paul didn't move. He stared at her back, struggling to separate duty from family.

Family won.

He jammed his hat back onto his head and grudgingly followed her outside, around the side of the house and into the backyard.

A field of golden wheat greeted him. Having grown well above his head, the stalks seemed keen on reaching straight for the sky.

"Stay close," Aunt Agnes said. She led him to a gap between the stalks.

He clenched his jaw, gritted his teeth, and rubbed at his nose.

Guarding her back, he followed her farther and farther away from the house. The wheat toyed with his growing unease, casting dancing shadows over his face and arms in the light breeze. He nudged the latch on his gun forward, curling his fingers around the grip.

The wheat ended abruptly, opening into a large clearing. In the centre, arranged in a precise line, Aunt Agnes' missing doors stuck out of the barren earth. A single rust-red handprint stained each one. They stood on their own like oversized dominoes—except for the last one. That door lay on the ground in several splintered pieces.

"Mystery solved," she said. She fisted her hands on her hips and glared at the broken door. "It would seem someone has interfered with my work."

Paul bit down on an oath. "What *is* this?" he asked.

Aunt Agnes pushed her glasses up higher on her nose and sniffed. "If you had stayed, you would know——"

"But I *didn't*," he snapped before she could finish. "For once, skip the guilt trip and tell me."

She stared at him until his nose burned. *Patience!* The word rumbled across his mind like thunder.

"I'm listening," he told her.

"This is how I keep him at bay," she told him, moving to the closest door. Little puffs of dust rose up around her shuffling feet. "The demon can move to and from our world using any door he pleases, locked or otherwise." She paused to look at him. "But you already know that, don't you?"

Paul said nothing.

"When he goes on the hunt for a new heart, I must lure him through a new door," Aunt Agnes said, moving to the next as if she hadn't just picked the scab of a very old wound. "I've been using my own blood to keep him contained. It's the only way to avoid offering him a sacrifice."

"Please tell me you're kidding."

"What did you think?" she asked. "That he would simply go away?"

"I don't know what to think," he said and pressed a hand to his head. "Maybe it's time you gave up the watch."

"How can I?" she asked, meeting his gaze. "There's no one left."

No one left but him.

He lowered his hand back to his side. "Will he come back?" he asked.

Agnes took a breath. "No," she said. "I'll make sure of it."

The way she spoke gave him pause. He looked closer and saw weariness in every line of her face. *It's not your fight,* he told himself, but the guilt was difficult to shake.

He turned to leave. "When it's done, call me," he told her. "I'll handle the other details." He headed for the cruiser and his waiting partner. Silently he added, *be safe.*

The rest of the day passed in a blur of evading pointed questions, lying on reports, and lying to his partner. When Paul got home, his head felt as though it had been run through a blender.

Turning the TV on, he found a random sitcom and leaned his head back against the cushions to watch. His eyes drifted closed.

He blinked — at least it felt like he blinked. Instead of his living room, he found himself lying in his childhood bed. His small hands toyed with the blanket pulled up to his chin.

"Mamma?" he called out.

It was a real dumb thing to say, especially when he remembered she couldn't answer. He'd been living at Aunt Agnes' house for over a month. He knew he would never get used to it.

The house was quiet and still. He could hear the steady drip of the broken faucet in the bathroom just down the hall. The warm glow of his nightlight was steady and strong.

He could see the little doll Aunt Agnes had given him. It hung on a thin metal nail from his closet door. Made of straw, it wore an orange tunic with a thin length of red string tied into a bow around its waist.

He glared at the ceiling. The doll was *supposed* to keep him safe. He didn't really see how. Not when everyone kept telling him Mamma was still out there.

"She loves you very much," Aunt Agnes had said. "But she loves magic more."

His nose itched. He gave it a good scratch and heard a knock from the other side of his closet door.

Goosebumps exploded across his arms and legs. "Hello?" he said.

In reply, the door rattled on its hinges.

Paul threw back the covers and raced toward the closet. He snatched the doll in one hand and was back in bed in the blink of an eye. Clutching the doll to his chest, he fixed his gaze on the still-rattling door.

The doorknob fell, hitting the carpeted floor with a dull thud.

Paul's eyelids widened. The door slowly opened. He thought he might wet himself as dirty fingers, with cracked and broken nails, curled around the frame. He saw a curtain of long, dark hair.

"Mamma?" he asked, unsure.

She looked nothing like the woman he remembered.

A pair of eyes peered at him through the greasy strands. One brown, the other icy blue.

"It is you," he whispered.

The gap in the door widened. His nightlight flickered.

"Paul-ieee." Her voice sounded nothing like her. She'd certainly never called for him in that breathy, high-pitched voice before. "Paul-ieee. Do you have a kiss for your mamma?"

His heels dug into the mattress and pushed until his back hit the headboard.

"He wants you, Paul-ieee," she told him, approaching the bed. "A little prick of the blade, and it will all be over." She grabbed his arm.

The doll tumbled from his grasp.

"You always were such a good boy," she said.

Paul screamed. He felt the blade slash across his forearm and caught the tangy scent of blood. He screamed again at the prick of her filthy nails digging into his skin.

"He Who Can Open All Doors," she called in that same high-pitched, breathy voice. "He who can give me the power I desire." She ran her hand over Paul's arm, smearing the blood from wrist to armpit. "I offer you my son."

The closet door slammed back and hit the wall so hard the plaster cracked from floor to ceiling.

The darkness inside the closet writhed.

A pair of yellowed eyes snapped open. They shifted and narrowed in on Paul before he heard the deep, feral growl that made the furniture rattle.

Too frightened to move, Paul felt something on the mattress bump against his free hand. His fingers found the doll. He gripped its tiny form until the straw crunched. Solid and real, the feeling of it gave him the courage to act.

He wrenched his arm away and scrambled out of bed. His mamma didn't seem to notice. Paul made a beeline for the bedroom door.

It slammed shut as if hit by a gust of wind.

"Paul-ieee," Mamma said. She plucked him up by the back of his pyjama shirt. "Don't you want me to be happy?" She lifted him, so she could look into his eyes. "Don't you love me anymore?"

"D-Don't *you* l-love *me*?" he stammered.

She didn't answer. "He Who Can Open All Doors," she called out, her tone now both harsh and shrill. "I offer you my son. Come and take him."

The dark continued to writhe as a hand, wide enough to palm Paul's head like a basketball, hit the floor. Long curved nails sharpened to points dug into the carpet. The yellowed eyes lunged forward into the dim light to reveal a face as red and raw as a burn victim. White-tinged blisters covered his temples and followed the sharp line of his cheekbones toward his nose.

Paul threw the doll. It bounced off the monster's forehead, landed on the floor, and disappeared beneath the bed.

The monster snarled and pulled his lips back to display a wide maw filled with rows and rows of needle-thin teeth. He reached for Paul.

His mamma laughed and lifted him higher.

The sharp points of the monster's nails touched the left side of his chest. Paul squeezed his eyes shut as they punctured his pyjama shirt. His skin.

The bedroom door exploded inward. Paul heard the monster roar before his mamma flew back. She took him with her. When they hit the ground, she knocked the breath from his lungs. Gasping, he managed to crawl away from her and slip under the bed.

"Enough, Imogen." It sounded like Aunt Agnes.

Paul peered out from under the bed and saw her. She stood in her nightgown in the bedroom doorway. Her hair cascaded down her back in loose waves. The light from the hallway made it glisten like threads of silver.

"Needs a heart, does he?" Aunt Agnes cried. "Give him yours!"

In three strides, she had Mamma by the arm and off the floor. It was then that he noticed the paring knife clutched in her hand.

"Blood for blood," she said in a low voice. The blade winked over the sleeve of his mamma's dress. Bright crimson seeped out to stain the edges. "And an eye for an eye."

Aunt Agnes pushed his mamma back. Paul watched her face contort into scowling rage, and then fear, as her feet slid across the floor. The muscles in Aunt Agnes' arm bulged as she sent her sister windmilling straight into the demon's arms.

He Who Can Open All Doors wrapped one hand around Mamma's waist and pulled her into him. The long nails of his other hand sank deep into the left side of her chest.

Aunt Agnes slammed the closet door shut. It rattled on its hinges. Lifting the knife, she stabbed the wood. It remained impaled there as she stepped away.

Everything went quiet.

Paul shrank back, watching her feet move toward the bed. A moment later, she lay down on the floor and reached for him.

"Are you all right?" she asked.

He nodded, even though he felt anything but fine.

She stroked the back of his small hand with her thumb. "Welcome to the watch," she told him.

Never, he thought, his gaze slicing past her to see his mamma's blood trickle down the closet door. *Never.*

Paul fell off the couch in his apartment, still feeling claw-like fingers pricking at his skin.

A buzzing sound gave him another good jolt, until he realized it came from the direction of his discarded trousers. He reached into the pocket and pulled out his cell.

"Frost here," he mumbled into the receiver. A quick glance at the clock on the TV told him it was three in the morning.

"*He's* here." Agnes' frantic whisper jarred him completely awake. "I can't——"

"Get out of there," he told her.

"Hurry," she said.

The line went dead.

Not today, he thought before he dropped the phone, yanked on his trousers, and snatched his keys. *Not again.*

Paul arrived at Aunt Agnes' house to find the front door and frame missing. The little doll lay face down on the porch. He snatched her up and stuffed her in his pocket. With a hand on his gun, he sprinted toward the back of the house.

The stalks of corn whipped against his face and hands as he ran through the narrow path. When he reached the clearing, he skidded to a stop. His limbs froze with a fear he hadn't felt since he was ten years old.

The front door stood upright next to the splintered one. Paul saw a pitch-black darkness in the centre of the wood.

The darkness writhed.

"I tried to warn you." The voice, horrifyingly familiar, jarred him back to the present. "Your aunt's a goddamn *witch.*"

"Hunter?" Paul said, shifting. He watched his partner step into the moonlight. Paul freed his gun and aimed it in Hunter's direction.

Hunter had Aunt Agnes by the throat. She wore her nightgown, her cat-eye glasses, and a fierce scowl. Paul spotted one of her kitchen knives clenched in Hunter's other hand. They stood only a few feet away from the door.

"You're not thinking clearly," Paul said. "Let her go. We can talk about this——"

"It took me *years* to figure out this particular puzzle," Hunter interrupted. The whites of his eyes glittered under the stars. "Do you think I could get anyone to believe me?" He raised the blade toward Aunt Agnes's neck. "I can't let you ruin this for me now."

Paul held the gun steady. Hunter pivoted and pulled Aunt Agnes in front of his body. The manoeuvre blocked Paul from getting a clean shot.

"I know it's hard to believe, but your aunt controls a *monster*," Hunter snarled from behind her shoulder. "She sends it off to do her bidding, to *kill* innocent people."

Paul's finger loosened against the trigger. "You don't understand —"

"I can prove it to you," Hunter interrupted again. His tongue darted out to lick his lips. "I released it. I released the monster. It told me what to do. How to stop her."

"You fool," Aunt Agnes cried. "The demon is lying to you!"

Hunter moved the blade closer.

"Stop! I'll shoot, I swear to God, I'll shoot you," he said, even though he knew he couldn't take the risk.

Hunter didn't listen. The tip of the blade pricked Aunt Agnes' skin. A drop of blood welled: a tiny, crimson bull's-eye.

Paul knew what came next.

A pair of yellow eyes appeared in the writhing dark. They lunged forward, revealing the raw red face. A hand followed. Long curved nails drilled into the dirt as its palm hit the ground.

"Here she is," Hunter shouted to He Who Can Open All Doors. "As promis — *aughhh!*"

Aunt Agnes bit his forearm. He dropped the knife and tried to pull away. Her teeth worked into his flesh.

Paul holstered his gun and ran, slamming into them. Aunt Agnes regained her wits first and dove for the knife while Paul wrestled Hunter to the ground.

"I don't have much time," he heard Aunt Agnes say.

Paul looked up to see her holding the knife. "What are you doing?" he said.

"He opened the door," she snapped. "That demon needs a sacrifice, and I won't make you choose."

He Who Can Open All Doors tilted his head in her direction. The hand bracing his body skittered to the side. He raised his other hand. Reached for her chest with his sharp nails.

Paul swallowed hard. *I won't make you choose,* she'd said. As if there could possibly be more than one option.

"You opened the door," he told Hunter. "You have to close it."

"P-Please," Hunter stammered. "He tricked me. He lied to me!"

"I can't let her die because you made the wrong choice," he said, his voice breaking at the wildness he saw in his partner's eyes. "Can *you?*"

"I can share," Hunter told him in a hurried whisper. "I'll give you whatever you want."

Paul snatched the blade from his aunt and slashed Hunter's arm. "Not on my watch," he said, and gave him a hard shove.

He Who Can Open All Doors wrapped his fingers around Hunter's torso. Paul knew the look of terror on his partner's face would haunt him for the rest of his life.

The demon pulled back and disappeared into the writhing dark.

Hunter screamed.

It was almost too much to bear.

"Finish what you started," Aunt Agnes told him, her voice soft.

Her words nudged him into action. "Blood for blood," he said, reaching for the door and slamming it shut. "And an eye for an eye."

He stabbed the blade, dripping with Hunter's blood, into the wood.

The night went still.

She clutched her hands to her chest before letting out a sob. "Oh, Paul," she said, and wrapped her arms around him.

It was a relief to feel her heart beating right where it belonged.

Paul took a breath, and then another. He wasn't sure what to do, but he knew whatever he said next meant everything.

"I don't know how I'm going to explain this one, but I need to call it in," he finally told her. "How about some tea?"

"I've got just the thing," she said, and led him toward the house.

THE BUMBLEBEE FLASH FICTION CONTEST

THE BUMBLEBEE FLASH FICTION CONTEST

Short, but oh so sweet, flash fiction is often the buzziest of literary forms. And this year's contenders for the Bumblebee contest were certainly a lively and entertaining bunch! Judge Bob Thurber had this to say about the finalists: *A fine batch . . . . All of them fun to read and so interesting to ponder.*

It was a battle of the 'bees to the very end, with 'Shayna's Eulogy' by Kate Felix just edging out runner-up 'Let's Start with the Horse' by Kim Martins, both described by Bob as *outstanding pieces.*

And we editors simply had to take another scoop. This year, the Bumblebee Editors' Choice goes to Mitchell Toews for 'Piece of My Heart'.

Thank you to everyone who submitted their flash. We can't wait to see what the hive cooks up for 2021!

THE 2020 BUMBLEBEE FLASH FICTION CONTEST SHORTLIST
    Elaine Crauder for 'Green, Green, and Green Again'
    Kim Martins for 'Let's Start with the Horse'
    David R Yale for 'No Shade'
    Meghan Romano for 'Parable'
    Mitchell Toews for 'Piece of My Heart'
    Kate Felix for 'Shayna's Eulogy'
    Natassia Orr for 'The Devil's Due'
    Hannah van Didden for 'The Slippery Man'
    Jacky T for 'Titrating'
    Kate Felix for 'Trudy Takes Charge'

Kate Felix (She/Her) is a writer and filmmaker based in Toronto. Her work has appeared in Room Magazine, Litro, *and* Cream City Review, *among others. Her feminist short films have been selected for over fifty independent film festivals worldwide and have won numerous film-making and screenwriting awards. Her small daughter describes her as being 'like a rainbow but with one stripe made of darkness'. Find her online at katefelix.com or @ kitty_flash on twitter.*

Kim Martins is from New Zealand and writes poetry, flash fiction, and short stories. For inspiration, she walks her two active dogs. Her poetry and fiction have been published in various journals: Barren Magazine, a fine line, Copperfield Review, Moonchild Magazine, VampCat, Flash Frontier, Fewer Than 500, *and* The Drabble. *By day she is a travel writer and editor for an online history encyclopaedia; by night she's at work on her first novel.*

Mitchell Toews lives and writes lakeside in Manitoba. His work appears in print and online, in places near and far. He is working on a novel. Mitchell's story 'Away Game' appeared in Issue 20 of Pulp Literature. *You may follow him on the trails or out on the water or ice, or more conveniently at Mitchellaneous.com, Twitter, or Facebook.*

Shayna's Eulogy

by Kate Felix

I'm wearing goth boots and ripped netters because screw you, sister, I won't dress down for your funeral.

Your mom is up there at the podium in her good dress. You know the one? Kool-Aid purple, three sizes too small? Remember it from when she used to go down to Hot Rocks to see if she could score you a new stepdad?

From the way she's going on, you'd think you and the baby Jesus were separated at birth. Get this one: "Shayna was always the first one in line to help out a friend." Yeah. Like the time we took the dirt bikes onto the golf course — one hundred percent your idea — and when the cops came you started crying and blamed the whole shit-pile on me? First in line, my ass.

She goes on about your bright eyes and shy smile like you were one of those apple-chewing brats on top of the fence post from her mother's fancy plate collection. Norman Rockwell special, that's you.

Right.

Like you never hung around with me and Orienta Esposito in the culvert drinking her uncle's Christmas rum from a mayonnaise jar? Like you never ran interference while I lifted a couple of packs from behind the counter at Kang's? Like you woke up every morning with the sun shining out from the backside of your painted-on jeans and never once called me up, high as Winehouse, at seven in the morning just to tell me how life is one big flaming joke?

How about that last time your mom came down to the ER and asked you how come if you wanted to die so bad you didn't just go ahead and do it? Not telling *that* story, is she?

Nope. Sorry. Can't do it, girl. I won't sit here with all of your stone-faced relations and listen while your mom pollutes the place with all that hot air. So, guess what, Shay? I've got a spray can in my pocket — it's yours, actually — and do you know what I'm gonna do? I'm gonna sneak out to the parking lot and write THE WORLD = A VAMPIRE on the side of that black car that's out there waiting for you.

Think of it, right? All your goddamn uncles in their boots and ties, gathered around saying, "Now who would go and do a thing like that?" I bet you'll laugh your face off down in hell just to look up at them standing around that painted-up creep-mobile, stunned as cattle.

But wait, what is this now? Looks like I missed my chance to slip outside because here comes your mom up beside me, and she's asking if I miss you as much as she does. Her breath is so heavy with Jack I can almost taste it on my own tongue, and it's making me think about the first time you and I got hammered and spent the morning face-planted on your back porch.

Remember how we woke to the smell of burning bacon and the sound of your mom hollering, "You girls get your delinquent asses in here and have some breakfast"? Remember how we thought the smell would make us heave? Turns out your mom knew as well as anyone what we needed to get past our first hangover, eh, Shay?

No. You know what, girl? Rewind. I'm not gonna let that one memory cloud over everything else that's happened since. So here goes me saying, "Excuse my French, Mrs Grenier, but she was a selfish little shit and it's no mystery where she got it from."

Except now I don't know what to do because she's gone quiet and all your uncles are looking this way. Can you help, Shay? She's got my face in her hands and she's looking so hard at me that something inside me is starting to burn.

"Sure," she's saying, "but do you miss her?"

And I do, Shay. Something awful.

But how can I tell her that when I can't even breathe?

Shay?

Why'd you have to go and do a thing like that?

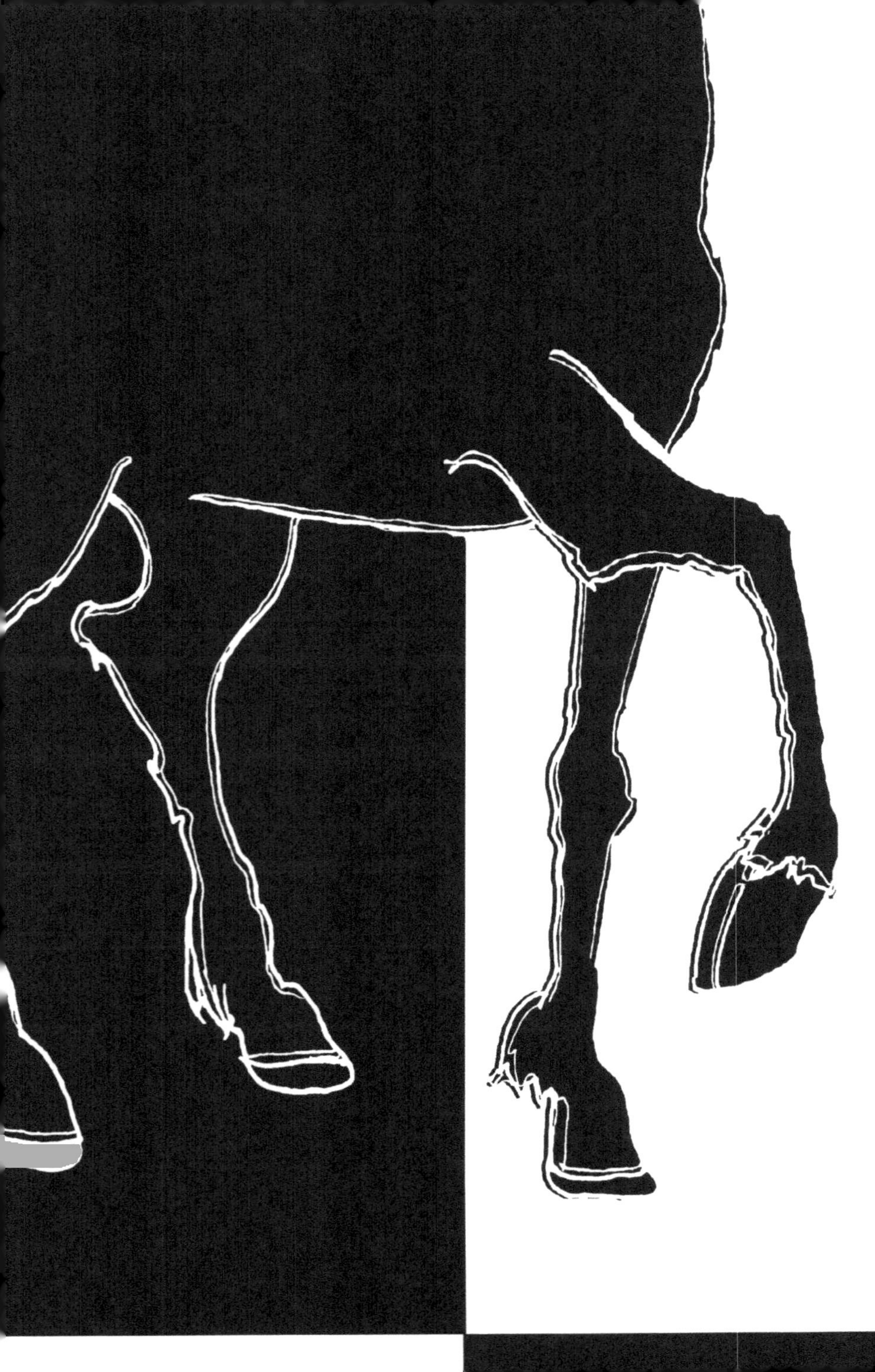

Let's Start With the Horse

by Kim Martins

A Ride in the Countryside

A white horse stands, its eyes dark as onyx, cows have their tongues to the grass, dogs are tumbling, clouds are like milk splashes. It's a Wedgewood-blue-sky day. I pedal fast past barns and farms. A long-rotten tree root snags the front wheel, hurtles me across gravel into a clump of bushes. Long walk back under ink-splotched clouds, a stinging wind slaps my face, restless rain soaks me to the bone, there's a pacing black stallion with moon-pale eyes, chained dogs snarling and snapping, cows with guns slung across their shoulders. There's been a change in the light, and I wonder what it will take to survive.

After I Left India

An official tells me at Tokyo airport that I won't be allowed to enter the country if I keep on refusing. I don't understand the shape of his words. His hands are like rice paper. He points to the machine with its black eye that doesn't blink. I shake my head, so they put me in a small room, no windows. I spend the hours considering whether I should have gone to Thailand, instead. I have not been arrested. Guess they can't be bothered because there's a hurricane coming, but that night I learned I could not run anymore.

I Think There's a Crocodile Behind Every Tree

We were paddling a canoe down the Limpopo: tangled jungle, dripping trees, strange sounds drifting. The streetlights weren't turned on. We wondered if we were good enough to eat. We built a campfire by the riverside, sparks spiralling skyward. A friend was missing, but we found him cursing and swearing under a fever tree, waving a knife and fork, a fearful crocodile clinging to a spindly branch. Now, I think there's a crocodile up every tree.

Halfway to Heaven

I was sliding through a Nicaraguan rainforest, filling my pockets with bleached bones and prayer books. A witch doctor showed me plants that cast spells, trees that walk and stalk your enemies. I considered swallowing them whole. An iguana monitored my heartbeat. The dogs were let loose from their kennels. Up ahead, a cross swinging upside down from a congregation of palm trees. Perhaps this is where they buried him.

The Woman Who's Not My Mother

Mum picks me up from school in the old black-and-white Zephyr. She tosses me a jam sandwich sticky with her anxiety, tells me we're being followed, to jot down the license plate number of the car behind. In the garden at night, she flashes the torchlight, searching for people who want to steal souls. She asks me whether I can hear the woman in the attic knitting, the clack-clack. Only four years to go before I can leave home.

No Big Bad Wolf

I was with Grand-Aunt Mabel at a riverside mansion that had a grand curved staircase, 'Daydream Believer' playing on the record player. I was dressed in a baby doll nightie, short with pink and purple frills. A palomino pony with chocolate eyes and a deer with antlers like corkscrews stood together at the top of the staircase. They were taking Polaroid photos of me. *All the better to see you with*, they said.

Piece of My Heart

by Mitchell Toews

On a still fall day, I walk through the woods near the river. My knee is behaving, and I work up a sweat under my Mackinaw. I come across an old campsite. A rusted stove, white enamel peeling. Tin cans in a pile. There is a blackened jackknife folded and set with care on a cushion of moss.

It's generations old, this place. The smell here is fetid and wild—no longer the stench of humans and the way we lay to waste and tame. We think we tame. Nature has reclaimed this antiquity with a bear hug of fresh growth and decay. Inevitability sits on its haunches near the long-cold fire pit.

But so too, this is the crude home where people like me and mine endured, fresh from a steamer ride across the brutish North Atlantic. My people, here in a sod-hut sanctuary where parents fed hungry children. Where families huddled, awe-filled under a blackout sky. Some evenings—and I can hear it and feel it, still present in today's silent hum—voices startle the quiet of the bush. Hymns sung with a fervour born of nothing left to lose. Eyes shine with hope in the glint of a midnight fire. There's the hollow, rhythmic clank of a spoon on a metal cup.

And the generations drew down and on, babies coming, some dying as they emerged, mothers staying teenagers forever. And slowly the black suits gave way to shiny belt buckles and plaid guffaws and soon TV antennas stood guard over prairie bungalows, their sin of worldliness now forgiven. "Billy Graham said so, Opa."

Now the politics and the lunatics are all together on the dance floor. *If only I could go back to the sod hut, or before that,* I think, a sip from my water bottle cool. *The miracle of science.*

I pick up a can, its label forty years gone, and it crumbles to red dust in my hand. Delicate fragments drop to the ground with the lightness of lace.

Reverent, I kneel and try to reconstitute the remnants, collecting them in a cupped palm. I make a sticky paste, adding dry grass and the blue of the sky and tears and a little bit of my heart.

"Come on, come on, come on . . ." I sing to myself, reminded of days hot with life, set on repeat in my mind. The woods echo Janis's howling refrain and I smell the fresh plastic signature of the shiny black LP held like a jewel in my hands, fragile and new and loud in my parents' basement. Stereophonic. Hi-fidelity. Hit parade.

"Best go back and get some goddamn work done," I say. "It's late, and I still have so much to do."

LINEN, LEEKS, AND BLOOD

Kris Sayer

Kris Sayer *has swum with dolphins, dived with sharks, hiked 'round 'Mount Doom', fixed a flat in the outback, eaten a ridiculous number of dumplings, and sketched more swords than you can shake an eleventh-century-blade-with-questionable-origins at. In between all those things, she's still made comics; 'Linen, Leeks, and Blood' is a prequel of sorts to her graphic novel* Tatterhood, *and it first appeared in* The Witching Hours *anthology. You can find all of her illustrated tales at wealdcomics.com, and pick up her comics and illustrations in* Pulp Literature *issues 1, 2, 5, 6, 10, 11, 15, and 21.*

OFR-HITI.
OFR-HITI.
OFR-HITI.
OFR-HITI.
OFR-HITI-OFR-HITI.
OFR-HITI.
OFR-HITI.
OFR-HITI.
STUPID OLD STUPID BODY...
...BEING ALL OLD AND STUPID.

—SOME...
SORRY, I HAD A FEELING YOU WERE SOMEONE ELSE.
crack snap
NOW THAT YOU'RE BACK, I NEED YOU TO GO INTO THE GARDEN TO GET—
OH.
inhale

HEALTH AND HAPPINESS TO YOU, OH GREAT WAND-CARRIER, I AM AĐÍSLA HRÍMHILDARSDÓTTIR AND I HAVE TRA-NO-JOURNEYED FAR TO ASK YOU TO TEACH ME IN THE WAYS OF SORCERY AND PROPHECY, I HAVE BROUGHT GOLD, GIFTS, AND-AND AN EAGER HEART AND OPEN MIND, IN HOPES OF LEARNING SPELLS AND MAGIC FROM YOU, MIGHTY P-PRACTITIONER OF, UM, MAGIC!

NOT AGAIN.
OH!
OH, PLEASE!! PLEASEPLEASEPLEASE MAKE ME YOUR APPRENTICE!! I'LL PAY YOU! I'LL WORK HARD!! I WON'T GET IN THE
GO AWAY.

THERE'S PLENTY OF VOLUR WANDERING AROUND OFFERING THEIR SERVICES; I IMAGINE SEVERAL MUST ROUTINELY PASS BY, BACK WHERE YOU LIVE.
BUT NONE OF THEM ARE A POWERFUL AS YOU!

I DON'T KNOW WHAT RUMOURS YOU ARE CLINGING TO, BUT–OOF–I DON'T KNOW WHY YOU THINK–
TWO YEARS!

...TWO YEARS AGO, I WAS HERE WITH MY–A WOMAN. SHE ASKED YOU HOW TO GET PREGNANT. SHE HAD GONE TO FIVE OTHERS BEFORE YOU, AND NONE OF THEM COULD HELP.
FIVE? HM, I THOUGH I WOULD HAVE BEEN THE THIRD.

BUT YOU KNEW. YOU HAD HER DO A RITUAL, AND IT WORKED. AND NOW MO–THAT WOMAN, SHE HAS TWO LITTLE GIRLS.
TWO? HM.
MM, I REMEMBER NOW. THAT FRIGID SNAKE WHO GOT ME DRUNK AND HAD ME SPUTTERING NONSENSE.

IT DOESN'T MEAN I'M A GRAND-HIGH SORCERESS. I'M JUST AN OLD WOMAN WHO KNOWS A FEW TRICKS.
SO SHOW ME! SHOW ME JUST ONE TRICK.
SIGH FINE. CLOSE YOUR EYES

click

HEY! THAT WASN'T MAGIC!
YES IT WAS. I DISAPPEARED. POOF. NOW GO AWAY

WHAT IF YOU TAUGHT ME JUST ONE RITUAL?
GO AWAY. YOU'RE TOO YOUNG FOR CHILDREN.
N-NO! NOT THAT ONE! WHAT...WHAT ABOUT A SONG THAT LETS YOU SEE THE FUTURE?
SONGS, VISION-CHANTS, BONE CASTING - IT'S ALL JUST FOR SHOW. YOU HAVE TO BE BORN WITH THE SIGHT. YOU CAN'T "SEE" THE FUTURE, IT'S JUST A FEELING YOU GET.
AND AS YOU GET OLDER, IT GETS WEAKER. LIKE I HAD THIS FEELING TELLING ME TO GO PICK THESE. COULD BE THEY ARE NEEDED FOR SOME DARK, MAGICAL PURPOSE...
BUT MOST LIKELY IT'S 'CAUSE THEY ARE NEEDED FOR DINNER.
...DARK MAGIC? ...LIKE, DEATH MAGIC? CAN YOU... CAST SPELLS TO ...KILL PEOPLE?
I...

I NEVER CAST CURSES OR BOUND WILLS OR DID ANY SPELLS THAT HARMED OR KILLED ANYBODY...
SEE? NOT A STRONG POWERFUL VQLVA NOW, AND NEVER WAS ONE.
BUT YOU KNOW LIFE MAGIC! SO...IS THERE DARK-LIFE-MAGIC? COULD YOU—
YOUNG LADY.
I'M OLD, WITH NOTHING BUT DRIED UP FART DUST IN MY VEINS. I'M NOT TEACHING ANYONE ANYTHING. GO BACK HOME, TO YOUR MOTHER, AND YOUR SISTERS, AND MAYBE IN TIME ONE WILL PASS BY WHO IS ABLE AND WILLING TO TEACH YOU MAGIC.
SIGH
THE HOUR GROWS LATE. YOU ARE WELCOME TO HAVE SUPPER HERE AND STAY THE NIGHT. JUST FOR TONIGHT. MY GRANDDAUGHTER SHOULD BE ARRIVING BACK SOO—

WE PLAYED TOGETHER, THOSE FEW SUMMERS AGO.
YOU REALLY DIDN'T TEACH YOUR MAGIC TO ANYONE, DID YOU.

THAT WON'T WORK AGAINST ME. YOU CAN FEEL THAT, I KNOW. EVEN IF IT DID, I HID HER BODY; YOU NEED ME.
SO...SHOW ME HOW MUCH POWER IS STILL IN YOU.
HOW DID ONE SO YOUNG BECOME SO STRONG?
I HAD FOUR EXCELLENT "TEACHERS". THEY ALL SAID YOU WERE THE MOST POWERFUL.
HAS SHE BEEN DEAD LONG?
UH, TWO HOURS? IS THERE A TIME LIMIT ON THE CEREMONY?
YOU REALLY DON'T WANT TO BRING BACK A DECAYED BODY.
OOH, SO, CAN...CAN YOU RESURRECT THE LONG-DEAD?
...
...CAN YOU!?

I-I HAVE TO HEAT HER HEAD UP...
...AND I NEED TO GET MY WAND.

YOU MEAN THIS? I'LL BE HOLDING ONTO IT.
...
BUT WITHOUT MY WAND...

YOU CAN'T DO ANY REAL MAGIC, I KNOW!
TOGETHER WE'LL BRING GRÍMA BACK!

JUST TELL ME WHAT TO DO, AND I'LL USE YOUR, UH, WAND.

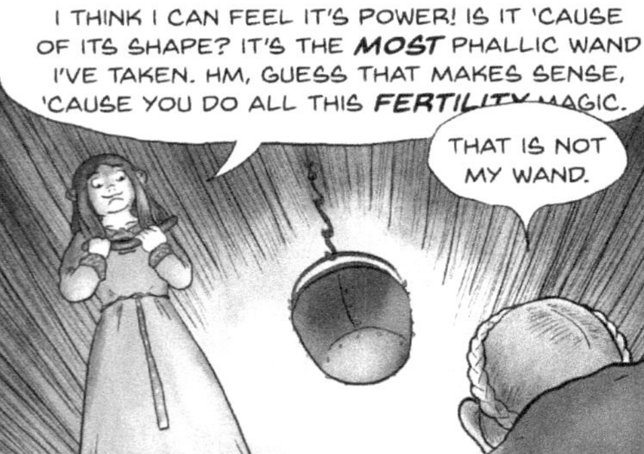

I THINK I CAN FEEL IT'S POWER! IS IT 'CAUSE OF ITS SHAPE? IT'S THE MOST PHALLIC WAND I'VE TAKEN. HM, GUESS THAT MAKES SENSE, 'CAUSE YOU DO ALL THIS FERTILITY MAGIC.
THAT IS NOT MY WAND.

YEEEECK.

AND YOU WILL NOT GET IT.

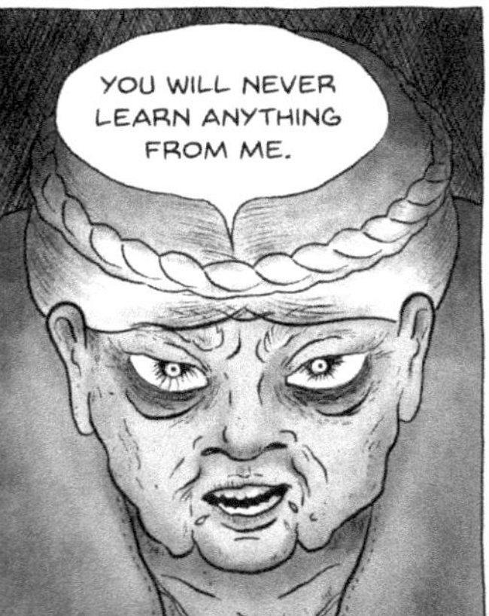

YOU WILL NEVER LEARN ANYTHING FROM ME.

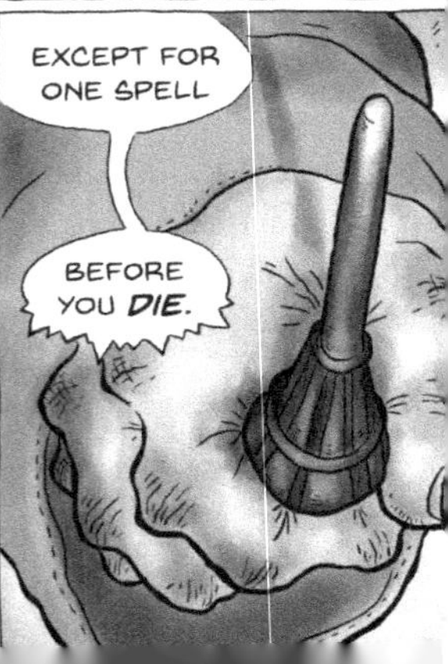

EXCEPT FOR ONE SPELL
BEFORE YOU DIE.

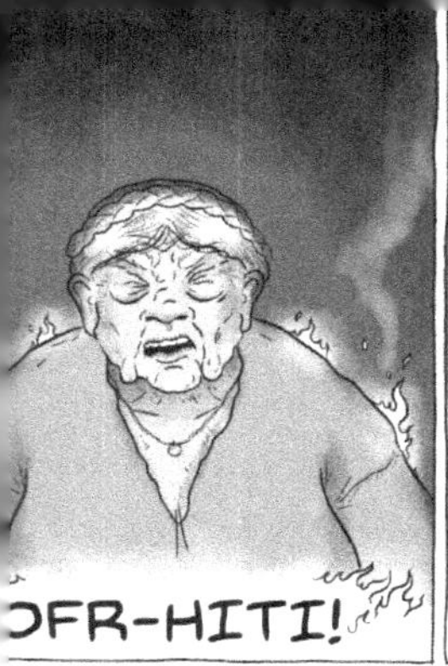
OFR-HITI!

OFR-HITI!

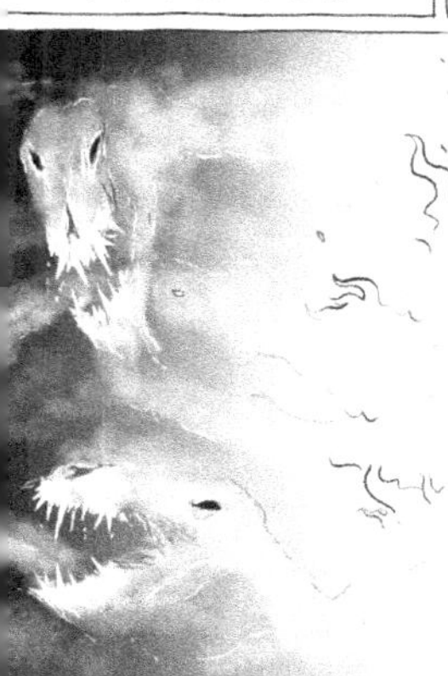
BROTNA!

AHA
AHA
AHA
AHA

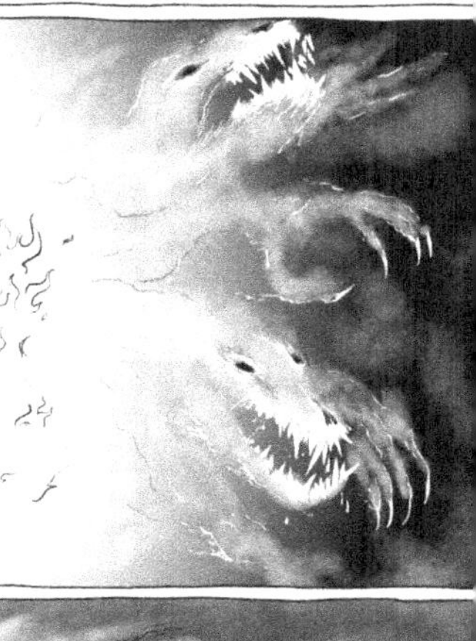
AHAHAHA

AHAHA
AHAHA

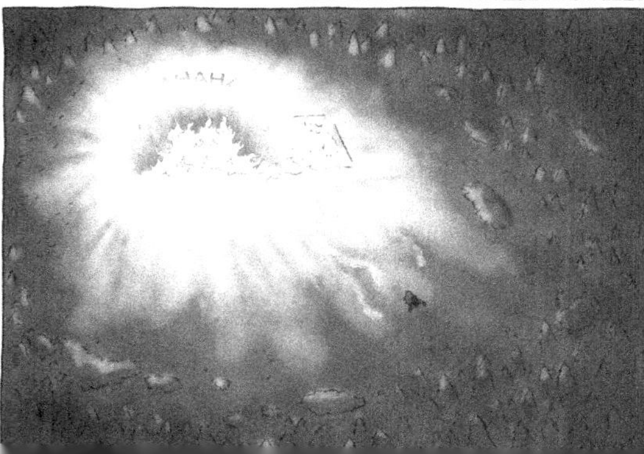

FRIGG!

LOOKS LIKE THIS OLD AND STUPID BODY WAS ABLE TO SCARE HER OFF.
SHE WON'T BE BACK.

BUT I KNOW SHE'S STILL OUT THERE.
A DARKNESS THAT WILL KEEP GROWING.

I'M NO LONGER POWERFUL ENOUGH TO STOP HER.

BUT I HAVE A FEELING I KNOW SOMEONE WHO CAN.

AMMA, CAN YOU TAKE ME OUT NOW?

ALLAIGNA'S SONG: OBURAKOR

JM Landels

Verse 1

Farewell and Well Met

It was one last chance to sing in the glittering great hall of the Bastion. How could I refuse? Tomorrow I'd be resigning my commission, but tonight was a time to celebrate.

I gratefully accepted the mug of pale cloudy beer offered me by a page, smiling to put her at ease as she struggled with her tray. She was younger than I had been when I first came here, and probably no less overwhelmed. "Thank you," I said, and lifted the tankard in salute. "A boon to a tired throat." We had taken this break, Kaelin and I, to rest our voices, but still had another set left to play.

She didn't leave. "Your singing is so pretty, mistress," she said, in a stronger voice than I'd credit an eight-year-old with.

Perhaps not as overwhelmed as all that, I thought. *Certainly braver than I was.* "Why, thank you," I reiterated.

"I want to be a singer," she said, scowling. "But my parents made me come here." The dislike of pagehood was evident in her face.

"It's not so bad as all that," I said with a conspiratorial smile. "I was a page here once too."

Her eyes widened. "Truly? Why aren't you a knight?"

"Not all pages become knights." I wasn't about to go into detail with this precocious girl regarding my banishment home to Teillai or my journey from there through the Ilmar when I'd subsequently run away from home. "I'm a Ranger. Or I was. I'm singing tonight with Mistress Kaelin before I bid farewell to my troop."

"Where are you going? Could I be *your* page?"

This girl was full of questions that I had no answer for, but the last was easy. "Rangers don't take pages. But while you are here, try to make friends with Mistress Kaelin." I nodded toward my friend. "She knows more about this land, its history, and its people than anyone else I've met. And if you truly want to be a singer, she is your best bet short of joining a Leisanmira caravan." I couldn't tell if the look on her face was fear or distaste at the mention of my grandmother's people. I hoped she would attach herself to Kaelin, who would educate that prejudice out of her.

Before the girl could ask more difficult questions, a senior page came up from behind and tapped her on the shoulder. She spun guiltily, splashing beer from the remaining two mugs on her tray, then managed an awkward curtsy back in my direction before hurrying off.

The senior page bowed. "Their Highnesses the Prince and Princess request your attention, mistress."

The beer turned sour in my belly. I had come here full of bravado, to perform in front of my grandfather incognito: a silent gesture of defiance after serving in his Rangers for six years without him knowing. Though I seldom used my spellsinging these days, I had done so tonight to alter my hair colour and the apparent shape of my face. Not, I felt, that Grandpapa would even recognize the twelve-year-old girl in the twenty-two-year-old woman.

I wound my way through the crowd from the performers' dais to the royal one at the opposite end of the hall. Grandpapa had his head turned, talking to a guest beside him, so it was Princess High Gwannyn who spotted me first. She had hardly changed in the years since I'd seen her, as if time had stepped around her while it engaged with Grandfather. He had always seemed old to me, as grandparents do, but the shock of the pouched skin around his watery eyes as he turned them to me made me stop where I was. I had wondered whether he would recognize me — it hadn't occurred to me that I would not recognize him were it not for the crown and the position of his seat.

Gwannyn lifted a hand. "Come closer."

I took a step nearer and bowed. "Your Highnesses," I said.

"The Prince and I have greatly enjoyed your performance tonight," said Gwannyn. Did she recognize me? I wondered. I had been beneath her notice until the day I was exiled from Rheran. Her eyes, as ever, gave nothing away.

Grandpapa was peering at me rheumily. "Gipsy," he announced. "Your voice is Leisanmira," he concluded, slurring the word.

Gwannyn put a hand on his, and the courtiers on either side of him turned to each other in polite conversation. He leaned forward, peering at me from under bushy eyebrows. "Sorry, that's not polite to say these days. But's true, isn't it?"

"Your Highness," I said, bowing again. "There is some Leisanmira in my family line" — *through your first wife*, I thought — "but I am, for the most part, Ilmari." Which was only barely true, for my grandmother was Leisanmira on my mother's side, and my unknown father was, if Mama had spoken truly, at least half Ilvani.

He leaned back on the throne, wine splashing from the cup in the hand which Gwannyn still held. She did not let go of his wrist. "I know you," he said. "I just don't know how I know you."

I lowered my eyes, adding a more rural lilt to my accent as I answered. "I've been in your Rangers for six years, your Highness." He would forgive me, I assumed, for neglecting to mention our relationship in front of his court.

"Well, your voice has made me happy tonight, young ranger, and I wish you weren't decommissioning tomorrow."

I felt my throat tighten, but I managed to answer, "Thank you, your Highness. It has been my honour to serve."

Gwannyn dismissed me with gracious words I didn't hear. I glanced up once more at my grandfather, but his eyes were closed, and his thoughts elsewhere.

The following morning my head was still muffled from too much beer, and my throat was raw from carousing. I managed to stay dry-eyed and dignified as a handful of fellow rangers and I accepted our medals, our scrip, and our thanks from the Prince himself. He was groomed and composed, and showed no indication of recognizing me. Yet when I shook his hand and accepted the purse of coins, I found a note in my palm.

So he had recognized me. And yet not a word of kindness or familiarity had passed his lips, either last night or now. I pocketed the note, determined to think no more about it.

An hour later I was in the stables with my bags tied to my saddle. I bridled my restless horse and led her into the yard. As I swung into the saddle, I gave a brief salute to the watchman, who opened the stable yard gate for me. No goodbyes here. I knew that whenever I was back in Rheran I would return for the bed, board, and company of other rangers. So many of our duties are solitary that we seek each other's company when we can. Ramira stretched into her ground-covering walk as we descended the streets of Rheran, her hooves echoing emptily on the dew-wet cobbles.

Once out of the city, I let the reins rest loose on the pommel as I pulled out my grandfather's note. *My dearest Allaigna,* it began.

It is one of my greatest regrets that I have been able to see so little of you . . .

Not enough of a regret to have made more effort than this, though, I thought bitterly.

. . . while all the while you have been faithfully serving your Prince and your nation as a loyal Ranger. If you are returning home to Teillai, please bear my fondest love to your mother, sisters, and brothers. I have missed too much of you all as you have grown

If you are not, however, en route to Teillai, I wonder if you are in need of a new commission? There is a hand-picked group of my best and brightest, which I will not name in a letter. They are soon to embark on an operation vital to the realm's security. You would be an invaluable asset to them if half of what I've heard of you is true . . .

What could he have heard in the time between not recognizing me last night and this morning? I wondered.

. . . and if all of what I remember of your indomitable character and keen intelligence remains intact.

Flattery won't win you loyalty at this late stage, old man, I thought.

If you decide to join this venture, details will be given at the rendezvous. If you choose not to go, I will think no less of you.

That was a challenge. He was baiting me.

Admittance to the meeting is by password. Yours is your third sister's second name.

That, I had to admit, was impressive. I doubt even their father knew my sisters' middle names, and probably would be hard pressed to tell which of the twins had been born first. It was this that swayed me. The thought that Prince Chanist, with all his affairs of state, had room in his thoughts for keeping distant grandchildren ordered and named, warmed me despite myself.

And then the pull to home was stronger than ever. To my mother and Angeley, to my sisters, with whom I'd never been that close, to my baby brother Vardry, whom I knew only as an infant, and even to Allenry. I made up my mind that home would be my destination. But the rendezvous point was on the way, and I was curious.

Grandfather's message said noon on the following day at a fishing village five leagues east of Rheran. I went early to the designated meeting point and obtained a modest plate of bread and cheese. Instead of wine I ordered watered beer — my savings would only last so long — and settled myself in a corner of the inn to wait.

Most of the clientele were fishermen, so it was easy to spot when the first member of the meeting arrived. He was Woodkin, tall and russet-bearded, and clearly ill at ease even in a village as tiny as this. I sank back in my chair and continued humming the tune that made me less noticeable. I wanted to watch and observe before making myself known. He said something to the innkeeper — his password, no doubt — and was directed to the far door of the inn room. There was still a quarter bell till the appointed time, so I continued to wait.

Next to appear was a knight. Not dressed as such, but evident in her bearing, accompanied by — and this shocked me — an

Ilvani woman. Soon after, a short, determined-looking woman entered and went straight to the room without speaking to the barkeep. This was the most varied patchwork crew I could imagine, and I wondered what exactly Grandpapa could mean by 'best and brightest'.

And then another man came in—so like to my former captain Chriani in face and feature that I nearly spat my beer back into my glass. Compelled, I rose and followed him.

I gave my password to the dour-looking man who opened the door.

"You're late," he said.

"I disagree," I replied as the town bell struck noon.

It wasn't the best way to make an impression, perhaps, but I was not about to let myself be intimidated. My eyes drifted around the room. Chriani's double, who had entered just before me, pulled a chair out from the large table for himself and hooked a second one with his ankle, pushing it toward me.

I nodded thanks and sat down between him and the Wood-kin. The Ilvani woman stared at me from across the table. Beside her were two men whom I had not seen enter—they must have been here all along. One was Mage Guard, judging from his garb. A shiver ran up my spine. And the other—I propped my elbows on the table and covered my mouth with my hands to hide my surprise.

He didn't show any sign of recognition. But I had changed in the eight years since I'd seen him last. I was at least a foot and a half taller, sun browned, and I had grown a womanly shape of sorts. Whereas he ... he was taller, broader of chest and shoulder, his curly brown hair cut short against his skull, and there was a thin scar on his square chin. But that full sensuous mouth and those large oak-coloured eyes I'd know anywhere. They belonged to my cousin Goff.

So stunned, so preoccupied by the coincidence that could not be a coincidence, for Grandfather would have known, that I hardly heard the mage begin talking.

"—handpicked," there was that word again, "by his Highness himself. That means I should have no doubts," his dry whisper of a voice paused as he scanned the room with thinly masked distaste, "regarding your abilities. Or fidelity. If any of you have any doubts yourselves about these things, you may leave the room now."

There was an uneasy shifting. Though I didn't want to be the one to speak first, it seemed no one else was going to. "How do we know whether to doubt our own abilities or not, if we don't know the assignment?"

Both Goff and the mage turned their stares on me. The mage's eyes I wanted to avoid, so I met Goff's. There was something different there—a puzzled look, as if my voice had triggered some remembrance, perhaps.

"She's right, Irnhad," he said, his lazy drawl deeper than before, but like enough to bring a wash of my own memories. "They have been told very little."

"More like nothing," I said, snapping more than I had intended. Why did the mage antagonize me so, just by his stare?

I leaned on the table, ready to push my chair back and leave. But I knew I wouldn't. Not without finding out why Goff was here, or learning more about the man beside me, who looked so much like my erstwhile captain.

The mage glanced at the door, and then around the room, waiting. When none of us rose to leave, he turned to Goff, and then the knight, who nodded. The knight reached across to the Ilvani beside her. There was a clinking sound and she passed a manacle over to Goff. My cousin locked it around his own wrist, and pocketed the key. The Ilvani stared straight ahead, her hostility a burning note in the air.

The mage procured a short rod, about a forearm long, and spoke an arcane word that set the hairs on my spine erect like a cat's. The sudden wash of magic in the room was oppressive. The man beside me stiffened, and I could hear his intake of breath. The Woodkin at my other elbow looked uneasy. The knight and mage rose, the latter passing the rod to Goff before leaving the room.

I could feel the tendrils of ancient, arcane power stronger than any I'd tasted before, rippling out from the rod. When I blurred my vision I could see its greenish smoky light wrapping around us.

The Woodkin stood, his eyes wide as a spooked colt's.

"If you're leaving, do it now." When no one moved, Goff picked up the long oilcloth-wrapped bundle from the table, stowing it under his free arm. "Then please," he said, "take up your belongings."

We reached for our various packs and cases, all eager to shake off the tendrils of arcana. Goff waited till we were standing, then snapped the glowing rod in two.

There was an explosion, soundless, or perhaps so loud my ears were overcome, and I felt myself rocked backward from the table, the chair behind me tipping as I fell against it in slowed time, and then blackness before I hit the ground.

Verse 2

Lost

There was a roaring in my ears, like standing too close to a waterfall. My tongue was dry and hungover feeling, though nowhere near so bad as my head. I tried to remember where I was, and kept coming up with a vision of Goff's — really? Was it Goff's? — face. The memories of the inn room were fuzzy and dreamlike. Perhaps it was a dream, for I wasn't lying on a wood floor. There was dirt, or sand, beneath my head. And the roaring — part of it was my ears, and the other part was a dry wind driving grit against my face.

I thought of Kîan, and the Sandhorn — a place I hadn't been for many years. But when I cracked my eyes into the red light of a setting sun I knew the sand and the light were the wrong colour. The air tasted wrong too. No hint of salt or sea, or even nearby fields or forests. Just the dry smell of dirt.

I forced my eyes wide open, pulling myself to sitting. A woman, some yards away did the same. She was one from the inn room. Not the Ilvani. Around us lay scattered bodies slowly being dusted over by the blowing sand.

Our eyes met, and the same questions crossed silently in the wind between us.

The woman and I mirrored each other's movements as we cast our glances around, at the orange sand-streaked horizon, the ruined stone pillars poking from the dusty soil, and the scattering of what might have been corpses lying around us.

We held each other's wary gazes as we checked our own bodies for injury. A stiff shoulder and a bruise on the back of my head seemed the extent of mine. The duffel in which I kept my bow and longsword seemed to have travelled with me. I remembered grasping the shoulder strap just before Goff broke the rod.

Goff. Keeping one eye on the woman who was rising and dusting herself off, I crawled the two yards to where Goff lay, handcuffed to the Ilvani woman. Would I be singing my cousin's death song tonight? I wondered. That would be too cruel a joke by fate: to not see him for eight years after parting on bad terms, and then to have him die before he even recognized me.

But there was a pulse throbbing faintly in Goff's exposed throat. He looked serene and more beautiful than ever, his sculpted features exquisite, despite the scars, under a layer of grey dust.

The Woodkin stirred then, followed by the thin, dark-haired man. Someone needed to speak, and with the only one who seemed to know anything still out cold, I reasoned it should be his next of kin.

"Do any of you know where we are?" I asked.

Three slow shakes of the head and confused looks were my answers. The thin-faced man, though, looked thoughtful and worried.

"What?" I asked him.

"Lothlecan," he murmured.

Lothlecan. My long-ago studies with my childhood tutor Willits had taught me about the elite guard of Imperial times, and my fireside talks with Kaelin had told me more. They maintained their hold on the Empire's far-flung reaches by wielding immense arcane power — the sort of power that had been abolished and forgotten in the wake of the Cataclysm.

I raised a questioning eyebrow, and he pointed past me. Turning, I saw on one of the ruined pillars the worn blades-and-crescent symbol of the Lothlecan.

But there were more pressing concerns. The Ilvani woman was face down in the sand, her arm twisted at an awkward angle by the irons which held her hand to Goff's. I was unsure how to roll her over without tangling the two of them further, but I put a hand to her throat, felt a pulse, and saw the movement of breath in her shoulder blades.

As I rose, her free hand snaked out and grabbed my ankle, throwing me off balance and onto poor Goff. I snatched her hand before it could do any more damage and twisted it into a none-too-gentle thumb lock.

"What was that for?" I hissed, repeating the question in Ilvani when she only glared at me.

"*Ildenoloth,*" she spat. The term has no translation, but is one of the worst insults an Ilvani can give.

Goff groaned, and I rolled off him, taking time on my way to kick the long bundle on the ground away from them. It clanked as I moved, and I felt sure it contained a sword or perhaps two.

The others watched warily but made no move to help or hinder.

"Goff," I murmured, nudging him with a toe. "Wake up, you jackass." I let go of the woman's thumb and stepped back, allowing her to twist herself to kneeling. I realized too late I should have removed Goff's sword and dagger from her reach as well, but she made no move toward them.

Goff swore. His eyes met mine, then flicked to hers. He swore again, sat up, and reached into his doublet pocket for the key to the manacles.

"I wouldn't," I advised, drawing my small sword and levelling the point at the base of the Ilvani's neck. "She's dangerous."

He looked hard at me, and I could see the thoughts colliding behind those liquid eyes. He still hadn't figured out who I was, and was wracking his brain for the connection through the haze of his recent unconsciousness.

"She is," he said, his normally fluid voice hoarse with dust, "but not to us."

He began to put the key in the lock, and I moved the point of my blade to a foot in front of his nose.

"I'd like an oath on that first, if it's all the same." I wondered just how long it was going to take him to recognize me.

He sighed, put his fist to his chest. "On my honour, as knight —"

I cut him off. "Not yours." *I know what your honour's worth,* I thought. "Hers."

I stepped slowly around them, the point of my sword inscribing a circle as I walked, till I was in front of her. I knelt and drew my father's bloodblade from my boot top.

Her eyes widened, and I could feel an uneasy shift from at least one of the other watchers. I took her cuffed hand, dragging Goff's with it, and made a nick in the thumb with the tip of the dagger, then smeared it along the length of the blade.

"On your honour, and your blood," I told her, "swear you shall allow no harm that you might prevent come to any one of us here. In your tongue as well as ours."

She did. "So be it," she finished in her accented Ilmari.

I wiped the blade clean without taking my eyes off of her, and slid it back into the scabbard in my boot. Goff unlocked his own wrist first, then hers. She took a moment to rub her forearm, and they both stood shakily. Then Goff made the mistake of turning his back on her.

In one motion she grasped the haft of his longsword and kicked him in the back of the knee. By the time he fell face first in the sand, she was standing with one foot on the back of his leg, and the sword point resting over his left kidney.

"Without that oath you'd be dead, *girdradhon*." It was an Ilvani word that translated roughly to *pigfucker*.

As tempted as I was to leap to my cousin's defence, I had too many questions — and suspicions — regarding his involvement in our predicament to take sides. The Ilvani and I eyed each other warily as she stepped over to reclaim her weapons, planting Goff's sword in the sand. I glanced at the others. The dark-haired man looked mildly amused and unconcerned. The short woman was ignoring us completely as she inspected her belongings. The red-bearded tree priest, however, was scanning the horizon.

He spoke, his voice deep and musical.

"Oaths and bloodletting will make very little difference if we do not find shelter from that."

He pointed across the featureless landscape to the swirling purple mass of sand gathering in the air.

It irritated me not to have noticed it sooner. Six years in the Ranger corps, living with the vagaries of weather, and it took a tree priest to tell me to take cover from a sandstorm. My friend Kîan had told me to find a rock, a promontory, anything, lie my horse down, and shelter between them. But we had no horses, and the standing stones were too narrow to hide behind.

The six of us stood, turning in place like clockwork cogs as we scanned the horizon for anything at all to head for. I looked down as well, hoping to see animal tracks, but the drifting sand had already smoothed out even our own footprints. The land seemed to slope downwards to the south — if indeed that was the south, and it was the setting not the rising sun to my right. Without any other direction to head, at least 'down' might offer eventual valleys or lees. I motioned to the others.

"This way seems promising — " I broke off, turning to my cousin. "Unless you know more than we do."

He shook his head, still spitting out sand. "Uncharted territory."

I turned to the Ilvani. "Do you see anything at all?"

She shook her head as well, but the dark-haired man pointed.

"Not sure if it's anything — but there's a smudge on the horizon there."

It was in the same direction as the downhill slope. Whatever it was, at least we'd get there faster than by going up.

Not wanting to see if they followed, I set off at a trot across the sand.

§

To be continued . . .

Allaigna's Song
Aria
JM Landels

Allaigna's Song
Overture
AMAZON #1 BESTSELLER
JM Landels

THE ARTISTS

Mel Anastasiou

Cover artist, Howe Sound Visitors; *in-house illustrator*

Mel Anastasiou loves drawing for *Pulp Literature* because she loves the stories she illustrates. She draws in black and white, working from imagination and inspired by details from Renaissance compositions. You can find more illustrations, as well as writing tips and news about her books and novellas, at melanastasiou.wordpress.com, and see her artwork on Facebook at Bird and Branch Artwork. Mel's cover painting for Issue 27, *Howe Sound Visitors*, was inspired by a speedboat photo odyssey near her Bowen Island home during one of the enchanted summers there.

Kris Sayer

Artist, Linen, Leeks, and Blood

Kris Sayer has swum with dolphins, dived with sharks, hiked 'round 'Mount Doom', fixed a flat in the outback, eaten a ridiculous number of dumplings, and sketched more swords than you can shake an eleventh-century-blade-with-questionable-origins at. In between all those things, she's still made comics; 'Linen, Leeks, and Blood' is a prequel of sorts to her graphic novel *Tatterhood*, and it first appeared in *The Witching Hours* anthology. You can find all of her illustrated tales at wealdcomics.com, and pick up her comics and illustrations in *Pulp Literature* issues 1, 2, 5, 6, 10, 11, 15, and 21.

HALL OF FAME

These are the heroes — the Patrons and Pulp Literati whose monthly support helped bring you this issue. Please lift your glasses and give them a rousing cheer!

The Shareholders
Rapscallion

The Brewers
Robin McGillveray

The Landlords
Adam Fout
A Bursewicz
Isabel Cushey
Dana Tye Rally

The Innkeepers
Ada Maria Soto
Margot Landels
Ev Bishop
Shannon Saunders
Roger & Anne Anastasiou
Kevin Harris
Gillian Gardiner
Megan Shaw

The Cicerones
Susan Lefeaux
Elsa M Carruthers

The Bartenders
Alana Krider

Richard Gropp
Ron Graves
Kristen Mah
Michelle Balfour
Robert Bose
Victoria McAuley
Dave Wayne
Scott F Gray
Abigail Bruce
Dietra Malik
Elaine McDivitt
Anna Belkine
Katriona Greenmoor
Famille Bussières
AD Bane
Multiverse Jumper
KT Wagner
Michael Weckworth
Terry Fries
Sarah Pendergraft
Deepthi Atukorala
Margot Spronk
Margaret Elliott
Bjarne Hansen
Iain Burns
Leny Wagner
Chris Olee
kc dyer

Jeffrey Parent
Kimberley Aslett

The Regulars
CC Humphreys
Marta Salek
Rina Piccolo
Jenny Blackford
Jain Cairns
Michael Barrie
Leo X Robertson
Kristene Perron
Akemi Art
Peter Halasz
BC
Miriam Zibkoff
Meredith Frazier
Heather Ane Wilkey
Catherine Levinson
Vera
Charity Tahmaseb
Alexander Langer

The Clientele
Ray Hsu
Melissa Hudson

If you would like to join the ranks of these worthies, you can become a patron on Patreon at patreon.com/pulplit, or join the Pulp Literati through our website at pulpliterature.com/join-pulp-literati/.

MARKETPLACE

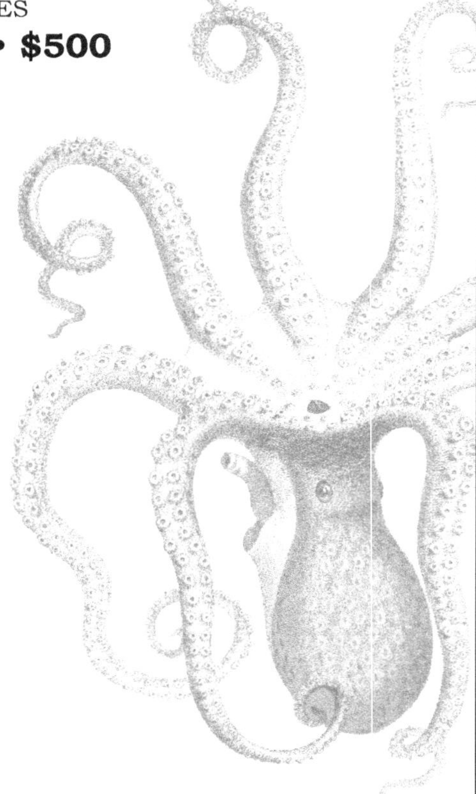

Do you have a **story to tell?**
We can help!

Dreamers is dedicated to heartfelt writing. Visit our site for:

- Therapeutic Writing
- Poems & Stories
- Content Marketing
- Creative Nonfiction
- Writing Workshops
- Contests & Anthologies
- Residencies & Retreats
- ...and so much more!

www.DreamersWriting.com

GEIST
go to geist.com/subscribe
or call 1-888-GEIST-EH
Keep it weird.
Subscribe today!
LOST CITY
FACT + FICTION • NORTH of AMERICA

onspec
the canadian magazine of the fantastic
Expect the unexpected.
www.onspec.ca

Allaigna's Song
Overture

J M Landels

PULP
Literature

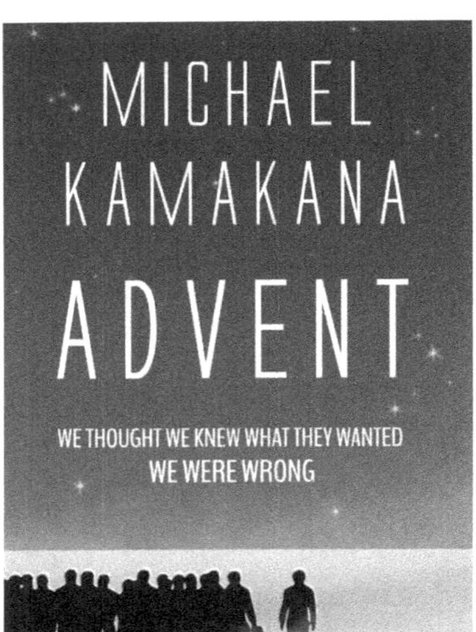

MICHAEL KAMAKANA
ADVENT
WE THOUGHT WE KNEW WHAT THEY WANTED
WE WERE WRONG

The Digest Enthusiast
Book Eleven
Jan. 2020
Steve Carper
Peter Enfantino
John M. Kuharik
Janice Law
Gary Lovisi
Paul D. Marks
Vince Nowell, Sr.
Jeff Vorzimmer
Joe Wehrle, Jr.

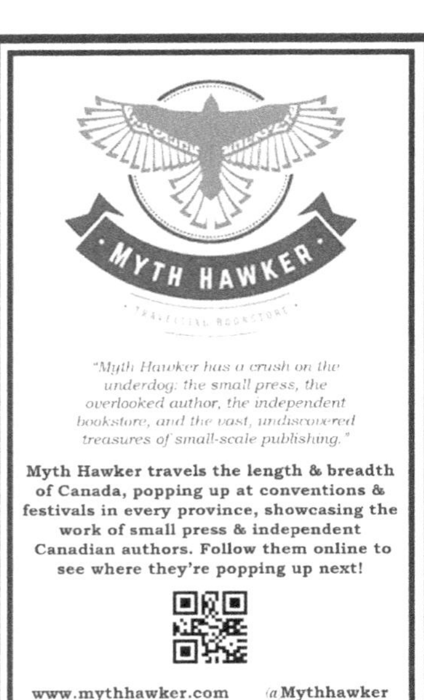

MYTH HAWKER
TRAVELLING BOOKSTORE

"Myth Hawker has a crush on the
underdog: the small press, the
overlooked author, the independent
bookstore, and the vast, undiscovered
treasures of small-scale publishing."

Myth Hawker travels the length & breadth
of Canada, popping up at conventions &
festivals in every province, showcasing the
work of small press & independent
Canadian authors. Follow them online to
see where they're popping up next!

www.mythhawker.com   @Mythhawker

JUNE 2020
MYSTERY WEEKLY
Magazine
Marshal Han was
wrong. Sometimes
evidence did fly
away...
Featuring
Tammy Huffman
Robert Lopresti
Arthur Vidro
Allan Durand
Luke Foster
Carl Robinette
Martin Hill Ortiz
THE CALCULUS OF
KARMA
by M. C. Tuggle

CONTESTS

Pulp Literature runs four annual contests for poetry, flash fiction, and short stories. For contest guidelines, prizes, and entry fees, see pulpliterature.com/contests.

The Raven Short Story Contest
Contest opens: 1 September 2020
Deadline: 15 October 2020
Winner notified: 15 November 2020
Winner published: Issue 30, Spring 2021
Prize: $300

The Bumblebee Flash Fiction Contest
Contest opens: 1 January 2021
Deadline: 15 February 2021
Winner notified: 15 March 2021
Winner published: Issue 31, Summer 2021
Prize: $300

The Magpie Award for Poetry
Contest opens: 1 March 2021
Deadline: 15 April 2021
Winner notified: 15 May 2021
Winner published: Issue 32, Autumn 2021
Prize: $500

The Hummingbird Flash Fiction Prize

Contest opens: 1 May 2021

Deadline: 15 June 2021

Winner notified: 15 July 2021

Winner published: Issue 33, Winter 2022

Prize: $300

$\mathscr{B}$ECOME A PATRON OF PULP LITERATURE

By supporting *Pulp Literature* on Patreon with $2 or more per month, you will be laying the foundation for a secure future for the magazine, as well as ensuring that you never miss an issue! Your subscription includes four big issues of short stories, novellas, poetry, comics, and novel excerpts, delivered to your door or electronic mailbox each year. **Find us at patreon.com/pulplit**

If you prefer to subscribe through our website, go to pulpliterature.com/subscribe.

Or you can send a cheque with the form below to
Subscriptions, Pulp Literature Press 21955 16 Ave, Langley BC, V2Z 1K5, Canada

Don't miss an issue!

☐   **Send me 2 years (8 issues) at the special rate of $90** (save $30)*
☐   **Send me 1 year (4 issues) for $50** (save $10)*
☐   **Send me 2 years of digital issues for $30** (save $9.92)
☐   **Send me 1 year of digital issues for $17.50** (save $2.47)

Name: ____

Address: ____

City: _________________________________ Prov. / State: __________

Postal code: ______________ Country:______________________

Email: ____

☐   Payment enclosed
☐   Bill me
☐   New
☐   Renewal

Make cheques payable in Canadian funds to J. Landels. Include email address for digital editions and Paypal billing, or subscribe at www.pulpliterature.com.

*for postage outside Canada add $20 per year in North America or $36 per year overseas.